Days
of
Wine
and
Rosaries

Fionnuala Carlin

Guildhall Press

First published in May 2009

Guildhall Press
Ráth Mór Business Park
Creggan
Derry
BT48 0LZ
T: 00 44 28 7136 4413
F: 00 44 28 7137 2949
E: info@ghpress.com
W: www.ghpress.com

The author asserts her moral rights in this work in accordance with the Copyright,
Designs and Patents Act 1998.

Designed by Kevin Hippsley/Guildhall Press
Copyright © Fionnuala Carlin/Guildhall Press
ISBN: 978 1 906271 20 6

A CIP record for this book is available from the British Library.

Guildhall Press gratefully acknowledges the financial support of the
Arts Council of Northern·Ireland as a principal funder under its
Annual Support for Organisations Programme.

ABOUT THE AUTHOR

Fionnuala Carlin was born in Derry and took a degree in English Literature at UCD before embarking on a vocational journey in Social Work. She is the proud mother of five 'almost reared' children who have inherited her deep love of literature and music. Her lifelong interest in writing has blossomed as her children have spread their respective wings to ply their own creative talents far and wide.

ACKNOWLEDGEMENTS

I am very grateful to Alf McCreary, mentor of the Dunfanaghy Writers' Group, for contributing the foreword to *Days of Wine and Rosaries*, my debut collection of stories. Also for his tutelage and guidance over the past six years and the craic and comradeship that has evolved from that.

I am deeply indebted to the staff of Guildhall Press – Paul, Declan, Kevin, Joe and Jenni – for their invaluable advice, professional guidance, and expert editorial and design skills.

I wish to acknowledge *Ireland's Own* and *The Canary That Did Not Sing* where some of these stories in earlier versions first appeared.

As ever, grateful thanks to my amazing family and friends for their honesty, support and encouragement.

FOREWORD

It is always a delight to introduce a selection of new writing, and I am pleased to have been asked to contribute this foreword.

Writing can be a solitary calling, which requires skill, commitment and, above all, an ability to focus. For some people there is nothing as terrifying as a blank sheet of paper, or an empty computer screen. My advice to all potential writers is simple: 'Don't talk about it, just start writing.'

Fionnuala Carlin, whose fine work is deservedly featured in this publication, has taken similar advice to heart, and now she can share in the collective and individual glow of those writers who see their names in print. This is not a totally new experience for Fionnuala, as part of her work has appeared elsewhere including the book titled *The Canary That Did Not Sing*. However, she has the honour now of seeing an entire publication devoted to her work and this is something which few enough writers have been privileged to experience.

In my long career, I have been fortunate to have written some thirty-seven books and countless articles for magazines and newspapers.

All of these have varied in their subject matter, but they have two things in common – each one has given me a sense of fulfilment, and I have always been aware that this was not the final word. The writing must go on.

So in that spirit, I congratulate Fionnuala and other talented writers of my acquaintance and tutelage. I hope that they will take to heart the message that the writing must indeed continue. This can be a journey of adventure and delight which will take them to places of creativity and achievement which they never thought possible, but they must never give up along the way! Fionnuala Carlin has kept on writing, even in the more difficult foothills of creativity, and she thoroughly deserves her success.

Alf McCreary MBE

CONTENTS

For my Mother
and Father
music when soft voices die ...

Resonance

It is corpse-cold on this mid-winter morning. The grass is a carpet of white frost, each blade of grass erect and frozen like a tiny petrified army. I pull my father's door quietly behind me, sealing in the warmth from the glowing range fire, and step out briskly, leaning into the biting north wind. The cortège waits silently as I make my way to the head of the procession and take my place behind the hearse.

'He's like his da, isn't he? Except he's not as tall as the big man.'

'Aye, right enough, he's the living image for sure. He's been away a long time; ye'd think he'd have been home before this, him being an only child and all. I heard he did all right in America, though. They say he was leader of a big orchestra out there and sent money home to the big fella religiously.'

'Sure, what good was that? He should have been here.'

'Ach, leave it out. The poor fella has enough to deal with today.'

The whispers find their way forward, borne on the wind like tentacles: accusing, comforting, questioning. I want to walk all the way to the church with him today. I need to remember, to feel him close.

I run through the order of music in my head, thinking what he might have chosen, wondering if I'll do him proud. My breathing quickens, the vaporised breath streaming into the cold of the day, threatening to leave me. I look around, desperate to focus, desperate to find ease. The place has barely changed in the twenty years I've been gone. I know each weathered wall and street and now recite their names over and over like a mantra, calming me, restoring me.

As we reach the chapel steps, I look up at the city skyline, jigsawed by ancient walls and single spires spearing far up into the clouds. This solid permanence loosens the noose around my throat and the memories come flooding back.

***

I'm six years old and holding tight my father's hand, feeling the tug and jerk of his wrist as I scamper beside him on the way to Mass. The cuff of his jacket bristles on the surface of my hand, back and forth as he stares steadfastly forward, his Wenceslas stride guiding and protecting me. Lights start to appear from frosted-glass windows like little low beacons in the dark.

We're nearly there on this lovely starlit morning and I begin to whistle *Silent Night*. My father joins in, whistling in harmony, and I'm proud of myself that I can hold my own note.

'Good little man,' he says when we finish, 'well done, but no whistling inside, now.' Then we're at the chapel steps and I let go his hand and hurtle towards them. A centre railing ladders the two flights of stone steps. I skip up the steps two at a time until I come to the top of the first level and then I'm snaking in and out of the railing, swinging head-over-heels on the bars, the dip and hurl making me giddy as my father watches patiently, hand at the ready should I fall.

He lights a cigarette then and I watch him as he leans back against the wall, one hand in his pocket. He draws the smoke deep into his chest, his face merging with the shadows. I can see only the white curling plume wisping into black, but sense the smile of his satisfaction.

'Only a week now till Christmas, Jack. I was your age when I first walked these steps with your grandfather. Did I tell you it was your granda who painted the chapel and polished all the wood and pipes of the great organ?'

'Did he play the organ like you?' I ask him.

'Better,' he says. 'He taught me all I know.' Then he reaches down and scoops me up, lifting me high on his shoulders.

***

At the bottom of the steps, the funeral director halts the cortège and asks who will do the first lift. I look around, deeply moved by the many hands raised behind me, and the task of shouldering my father to the church begins.

The relays overlap seamlessly. At the church door, I take my place beside the coffin, waiting for the priest to bring us forward. My eye is drawn to the stone-pleated water font at the entrance to the organ-gallery steps and I'm back in the December morning of long ago.

***

'Bless yourself now and tell Him you're here,' my father says, lifting me up to dip my hand in the soaking sponge, heavy with Holy Water.

'Morning, Jesus. This is me: Jack.'

'Good boy,' he says, fishing the great bunch of keys from his inside coat pocket, which he jangles a number of times before finding the key to the organ-gallery door. The chapel is empty except for the baby Jesus in his tabernacle. I love the word tabernacle and say it over and over. It rolls off my tongue like honey. 'Say your prayers now, Jack,' my father says, 'this is your special time with Him before all the people come in.'

He kneels beside me at the front of the choir seats, his head in his hands. I can see through his fingers that his eyes are closed and his brow all crinkly. I copy him, watching through my fingers until he looks up and blesses himself, then I do the same. When he stands up, I have to stretch my neck to look up at him. His glasses have steamed up and he takes them off to wipe them with his white hanky, which has the letter P marked on it. 'What does the P mean?' I ask him.

'Perfect,' he says, the hint of a smile on his face.

My father rolls back the organ lid and carefully runs his hands over the silent keys. 'Come here, Jack,' he says, twisting round to lift me up beside him. 'Okay, what do I do now?' he asks me.

'Blow up the bellow,' I say, proudly remembering the right words.

'Good boy. Now show me which key to press.' I reach forward and flick the switch. Suddenly, the organ comes to life. The bellows whoosh and sigh, sending warm draughts of dusty breath far up into the great brassy crown of pipes above. 'See that, Jack? He's wakened up; all he wants to do now is sing.'

'Can I pull out the plugs now, Da?'

'Not plugs, son; these are called stops, but I'll teach you about that later. Now, down ye go and wait and I'll call you up when the choir comes in.'

He lifts me down, then shuffles himself to the end of the seat and into the organ wings where he begins to leaf through the sheets of music for the morning's Mass. I watch him for a moment before I run to the front of the gallery, skipping along the flat broad steps until I reach the end and look over. I have to place my arms on the cream curving scroll and heave myself off the ground to see the floor beneath. The people are just starting to arrive. A cold blast of air scissors upwards from the floor below. I wave down to my aunties, Mary, Rose and Jean, who sit in their usual seat by the confession box.

Mary takes out her hanky and waves up to me with a big fat smile; she has tiny hairs coming out of her chin and a lovely pair of blue eyes. Dad says Mary is special to God and will go straight up to heaven. I worry about that because she's so fat. I'm not sure the cloud will hold her, but Dad says when you die you're as light as a feather. I like Mary: she smells of tobacco and soap and she has a wooden donkey that fires cigarettes out of its tail.

Rose is reading her prayer book, mouth moving as she smiles up at me and nods.

Jean looks up now and frowns at me before taking Mary's hanky and putting it firmly in her pocket. I hide behind the pillar. Jean is very, very holy.

I fall into a daze now as the smoke from the candles blurs the scene below. James the sacristan is clumping over the altar steps, lighting the tiny flames, head bent in solemn concentration. In the sacristy, James can pull a switch that controls the lights above the organ and lets Dad know when the priest is ready to come onto the altar.

Back up at the organ, my father is pulling out the stops – the thump and click of them sounding like shiny snooker balls colliding – then stretches out his feet to engage the bass-pedal notes.

The pedal notes hum grumpily, like Edward, who sings the very lowest notes in the choir. Edward has a voice that starts away down in his shoes and climbs like a beanstalk up into his throat.

Then Dad strokes the polished black and white keys lightly, crossing his hands one over the other, making little angel sounds, just like the angels my grandfather has painted high up in the corners of the ceiling. The sweet sound echoes through the pipes and reminds me of Peggy, who sings all the top notes. She's like a little china doll, all pointy and shiny. Peggy and me always play a game before Mass. I tell her my father says she's not the size of tuppence.

Peggy winks at me and takes her hand from behind her back, each fist tightly closed. 'Well, Jack,' her voice is low and gravelly, not a bit like her singing voice, 'which hand?'

I pretend to think hard and try to open the fists, but Peggy is strong, even though she's just the size of tuppence. 'Right one,' I finally say.

She opens her hand and there, sure enough, are two bright shiny pennies. 'There's tuppence for ye!' she says, throwing back her head in silent laughter.

***

I close my eyes now as the priest intones the funeral prayers before us. I follow the coffin to its central resting place before the altar, then turn down the left-side aisle and begin to mount the steps to the organ gallery.

My footsteps echo in the acoustic of the stairwell, staccato sounds, thudding alongside my heart. By the time I reach the top, beads of sweat have erupted on my forehead. The priest has gone into the sacristy now to prepare for the Requiem Mass.

I sit on the organ seat, facing the colonnades of fluted plaster each side of the magnificent altar where great gold letters spell out the words Glory To God On High. Then I swing round, flicking the switch, pulling out the stops: the stopped diapason, vox humanae, principal, flute, tierce, cornopean, swell-to-great coupler and pedal diapason, their names lovingly taught by my father now resonating, vibrating in my memory. I stroke the keys on the two-tiered console, watching my hands – seeing my father's – flex and close, poised to play.

14

His dream was a simple one: that my musical footsteps might echo his as he had followed his father's. He had never complained, his letters full of encouragement, praise and love, and pride in my chosen path.

A silver tear rolls down my cheek.

The great organ has lain silent in this beautiful old church since his retirement.

Now the swell builds and the great bass groans; the reed pipes fill with glorious air in joyful expectation. I nod to the choir as the gallery lights flash above my head and, with a heart full of love, play my father home.

DAYS OF WINE AND ROSARIES

'Would you look at that!' The nurse smiled broadly as she peered into the commode. 'Good girl, Marnie, a great result,' she added, lifting out the pan and deftly covering it with a paper towel. Marnie was bent over, leaning on the handles of the commode, one grey stocking crumpled sadly around her ankle.

'Come on, now, that's a girl, fix your skirt,' said the nurse, both hands now occupied as she supported Marnie.

'Result?' Marnie warbled, her voice tremulous as froth. 'Are the results in?'

'Just fix your skirt, now, Marnie. Come on, reach round and pull it down, you can do it. Good girl,' the nurse said, trying to balance with difficulty as Marnie leaned back on her.

'Where's my skirt?' Marnie said, stretching out her hand aimlessly. 'Where did I leave it?' she asked, making to sit down again.

'It's on you, Marnie.' The exasperation in the young woman's voice was lost on Marnie, who looked up at her, bewildered.

'What's on me?'

'Oh, for goodness sake!' shouted the nurse, the strain of balancing the pan and Marnie becoming too much. 'Here, move round a bit,' she said, biting her lip in concentration as she stretched out to grab hold of the skirt.

Unfortunately, Marnie chose that same moment to swing around, too, causing the girl to overbalance and drop the pan. 'Oh, my God!' the nurse cried as the subject of the recent celebration shot sloppily over the polished linoleum floor.

Marnie started to laugh, a high-pitched giggle, as the nurse quickly adjusted the clothes and led her back to the sitting room. 'God give me strength,' the nurse muttered, her face a rictus of restraint.

The only other trained staff nurse hadn't turned in that day; still, only another hour before the night shift would relieve her. It had been a long day. *Thank God the numbers were well down*, she thought. *A few deaths made all the difference.* Helping Marnie into her chair, she looked across at the two other residents, whose benevolent expressions summoned an unbidden thought to her mind. *People are living far too long these days. Mind you, these three are in a class of their own: all as mad as March Hares.*

'I'll have to get this cleaned up now. I'm on my own today, girls, so no more requests; you'll just have to wait. What is it, Jane?' she exhaled loudly, dragging her hand through her hair.

Jane, a white-bunned little lady, sat very straight in her chair, feeding her rosary through her fingers. The beads, which she maintained came from the pope himself, lay over the grey nun's habit of her own designing. Her hand was raised in question. 'I need to get the vestments ready for Mass.'

'I told you before, Jane, this isn't the chapel. Now just sit quiet there until I get back.'

'Can I have a sherry?' asked Marnie, inclining her head towards the dark walnut sideboard where the sherry bottle and three dainty glasses sat on a silver tray.

'You know you don't get sherry until dinnertime, Marnie.' *I could do with one myself; roll on the happy hour.* 'Now, no more questions until I wipe up this mess.'

After the job was done, the heavily built nurse, face flushed with exertion, walked briskly through to the adjoining room to check on her other residents. Marnie waited until she was out of earshot, then whispered to Cassie and Jane, 'That big girl must be new. I haven't seen her before.'

The two ladies stared ahead, Jane reciting her prayers with perfervid concentration and Cassie humming gently.

After a while, Jane's chanting stopped. 'Who's that wee critter over there?' She turned to Cassie, pointing up to an image of the Sacred Heart. 'He's been sitting up there all day, looking over at me and not saying a word.'

'Seven o'clock,' said Cassie, smiling benignly.

Marnie, meanwhile, was concentrating on her loosened stocking. The marked curvature of her spine made it uncomfortable for her to raise her head, reducing her vista, in the main, to floor level. With painstaking patience, she now pulled at her stocking until it came off. Then, very slowly, she began folding it over and over in perfect little symmetrical shapes until she was left with a small, fat triangle of silk. She drew it gently across her face, glancing at her two companions before concealing it neatly inside her thermal vest.

'The school bell's very late today,' Marnie said. 'I wonder where my class has gone. I need to get them ready for the inspection. Oh, Lord, I nearly forgot about the medical inspection. Is it today?' She leaned over towards Jane.

'Nurse Pitts has fits when she sees nits,' lilted Jane, her hooded eyes bloodshot against her dough-white skin.

Cassie raised herself straighter in the chair, her fingers steepled as she nodded. 'Nit, the egg of the head louse, *pediculus humanus capitis,*' she said, 'feeds off the blood on the scalp. Nasty little creature. I saw a child in my surgery yesterday; the poor mother was distraught because the child was having repeated episodes.'

Cassie sighed and raised a hand to her temple. The tiniest grace note of a frown began to furrow her distinctive brow. 'Who are those children in the corner?' she suddenly asked.

Jane started forward. 'Oh, good, good.' She clapped her hands.

'Is that my class? Where are they?' lamented Marnie.

'They're over there, jumping up and down,' Cassie said.

'I can't see them,' Marnie wailed. 'They'll be late for the inspection.'

Jane was up from her seat now, swaying and singing at the top of her voice.

'What's going on here?' the nurse cried, clapping her hands authoritatively as she strode briskly back to the room.

Marnie was halfway to her feet, her body bent at an angle of forty-five degrees. 'Get over here, girls,' she warbled. 'The inspector's coming.'

Jane was reciting the rosary, eyes lifted to heaven as the nurse looked at the scene before her with mounting impatience.

'Sit down, Marnie. God of almighty, what's going on?' she cried.

'It's those children in the corner,' said Cassie.

'Now, Cassie, I've told you before. There's only you, Marnie and Jane.' She enunciated each word in clipped tones. 'You're all in the Nursing Home; this is your home now. There are no children in here,' she said forcibly.

'Oh, but there are,' insisted Cassie. 'Over there in the corner.'

'Look, Cassie,' said the nurse, moving over to the corner where she began flapping her arms up and down, 'there's nobody here. It's all in your head.'

Cassie sat back, a secret smile on her face.

'Now settle down, the three of you,' pleaded the nurse, kneading her fist against her throbbing temple. *My blood pressure must be through the roof.* 'Marnie, where's your stocking?' she demanded. 'I've told you a hundred times about hiding your clothes.'

'Not telling,' Marnie giggled, putting a finger to her lips.

'Marnie!' the warning voice repeated.

Suddenly, Cassie burst out laughing. 'Fooled you, fooled you,' she shrieked. 'They're in the other corner.'

Jane now joined in. 'Nurse Pitts has nits. Nurse Pitts has nits. Hail Mary, full of grace, have you any wool?' she chanted, clapping her hands.

For a brief moment, the nurse thought she would join them; she was losing her reason. *Where the hell was the night shift?* 'Stop it! Stop it!' she shouted out loud. 'Marnie, where is your stocking? I know you've hidden it again. Where is it? Give it to me now … or no sherry tonight.'

Suddenly, it all became too much for the distraught nurse. 'Keep quiet, you raving lunatics!' she roared. 'Shut up!'

Cassie stopped laughing immediately, the expression on her face lifting as though a blind had been drawn back. 'Don't shout, Nurse,' said Cassie, 'we can hear.'

'Marnie, give the nurse your stocking, you'll get a cold. When you have a moment, Nurse, she could do with a blast of her nebuliser. She was a bit wheezy during the night.'

The nurse, who had been caring for Cassie for two years, now recognised one of the elderly doctor's rare pockets of lucidity and, with all the skill and wisdom of her vocation, eased back from the edge of her intolerance. 'Sorry, Cassie. I'm under pressure here today. Staff shortage and all. I'll see to it in a minute … when I get a chance,' she added as Marnie produced the stocking, pulling down her vest and exposing the criss-cross welts of a primitive mastectomy.

'Good girl, Marnie,' she said now. 'Let me fix your blouse,' she added gently, never failing to be touched by the old lady's scars. *Thank God for modern medicine*, she thought, *the old girl has done well to survive. I'd better be careful with my temper and go easy on them. Though God knows they'd put you astray in the head.*

She leaned on the edge of the chair now to lever herself down to her knees and replace Marnie's stocking, just as the dinner bell rang from the kitchen.

'Jesus, Mary and Joseph, it's Mass time!' Jane called out, rising from the chair and reaching for her stick.

'What's the time? Is that the time? Oh, my God, he must be here. I have to go, I have to go,' said Marnie, all her limbs now moving as though commanded by an invisible puppeteer.

'Stay at peace, Marnie, till I get this on,' muttered the nurse between clenched teeth, at the same time reaching over towards Jane. 'Jane, sit down, you're going to fall,' she cried as Jane teetered precariously above her.

Just at that, Marnie shot forward in her seat, her forehead clashing against the nurse's bent head. The force of the blow unbalanced the nurse, who fell back awkwardly, her head snapping upwards, just as Jane finally lost her balance and fell heavily on top of her with an ominous crack.

'Goodness gracious!' exclaimed Cassie. 'Are you all right?' She leaned over to where Jane lay winded, the bent legs of the nurse splayed beneath her. Marnie sat immobile in her chair, her eyes closed. 'Nurse, are you all right?' Cassie called, tentatively at first, then louder. 'Nurse, Nurse, can you hear me?'

Reaching for her Zimmer frame, Cassie struggled painfully to her feet, shuffling the two or so paces to where Jane lay. Surveying the scene, with the fading practised eye of her late profession, she began to prod Jane with her shoe in an effort to bring her around. Getting no response, she moved slowly over towards Marnie and, reaching down, shook her – gently at first, then with more urgency.

'Marnie, do you hear me? Marnie, open your eyes.' She bent over then and placed her hand on Marnie's forehead; an angry bump was emerging from the pallid skin. *Better out than in*, she thought. Then, hearing the gentle susurrus of her snoring, Cassie realised that, at worst, Marnie would have a bad headache when she woke up. She stood for a minute, unsure of what to do next. Clouds were beginning to form again; her head felt a little fuzzy. She knew there was something else she should be doing, but for the life of her didn't know what it was.

Cassie shuffled back to where Jane lay now moaning. 'Hold on to this and help yourself up,' she told Jane.

'Where am I?' said Jane.

'You fainted, dear,' Cassie could hear herself say, although she had no idea what this meant. Her anxiety was rising as she tried to claw back the dissipating threads of her memory.

Fainted. The word seemed alien to her. 'Faint, fainted, simple faint,' she called out loud as Jane rose to her feet, clinging on to the Zimmer frame.

'Faith of our Fathers, Holy Faith,' sang Jane.

'Faith,' echoed Cassie. 'Faith? Faint? Faith … yes, that's it,' she said uncertainly.

The nurse lay on the ground, her head at a funny angle, a small trickle of blood escaping from her ear.

Marnie now stirred in her chair, lamenting, 'What time is it? My head hurts,' she cried, her voice shaky, a breath away from tears. 'Is it time for sherry?'

Jane was still leaning on the Zimmer frame, looking down at the nurse.

'Tut, tut,' she clucked, her head shaking from side to side. 'She's drunk … and in the chapel, too. She should be horsewhipped.'

Cassie looked down at the body on the ground with curiosity. *What was it that she should do?* she wondered.

Marnie was up on her feet, lurching sideways towards the sherry bottle.

'I think …' said Cassie, 'I think …' she said again, but

nothing else came as she succumbed to the cocoon of the clouds, a slow smile spreading across her face. 'I know,' she laughed. 'Let's hide.'

Jane clapped her hands. 'Hide and seek, hide and seek,' she sang.

Marnie had no idea how to get the sherry from the bottle to the glass. And so, with a mighty effort, she began swigging the amber liquid as her two friends, attached to their Zimmers, shimmied towards her.

'It's the happy hour,' cheered Cassie, lifting the bottle from Marnie and passing it to Jane, who blessed herself reverentially before downing a mouthful.

Marnie was bent over again, her head bobbing, as though disconnected from her body.

'Is it my turn again?' she asked Jane, who hiccoughed before passing the bottle back to Cassie.

'You're next,' giggled Cassie, hoisting the bottle to her lips and closing her eyes as the golden liquid coursed like nectar down her throat.

'Happy hour,' she cheered as the sounds of the nightshift approached in the distance.

'Hide!' squealed Jane. 'Hide and seek!'

With Marnie clutching the bottle and clinging precariously to the Zimmer, the trio now shuffled tipsily behind the sideboard and sank bonelessly to the floor in a tangle of arms, legs … and rosary beads.

A Social Service

Hannah Carton's first day at her new job began with a series of unfortunate events. The bus, always fairly reliable, was running late. The new navy trouser suit she had bought when she was half a stone lighter had popped a button as she stooped to tie her shoelace. And as she fiddled with a pin at the bus stop, a lorry driver travelling in the opposite direction took his bend too fast and skidded, spraying the waiting bus queue, and Hannah, with a wave of filthy water.

Still, as she climbed the stairs to the Social Services building, Hannah was determined, despite her now less-than-satisfactory appearance, to create as good an impression as possible.

'Can you tell me where I can find Mr Paul Clarke?' Hannah asked, smiling at the blonde-haired receptionist, who was typing furiously, tongue protruding in serious concentration.

Without looking up, the girl nodded her head in the direction of the door to her left. The title on the door read: Miss Estelle Hogg – Senior Personal Assistant. *Grand title*, thought Hannah, eyebrow raised as she knocked at the door.

'Come in!' an imperious voice commanded.

'Hello,' smiled Hannah, taking in at once a snapshot of a moon-round face with large bulbous eyes and what could only be described as 'old hair', wiry and unruly, like too many perms gone wrong. *God forgive me*, thought Hannah wickedly as her smile widened, *she's like a telly-tubby granny.* Hannah's smile vanished, however, as the woman before her stood up, her eyes cold. She didn't speak a word as she scrutinised Hannah from the bottom of her feet to the top of her head with overt disdain.

'You're the new social worker, then?' She raised her eyebrows with distaste and once more her eyes travelled over Hannah, settling on the muddied trousers. 'I hope you dress more like a professional befitting your title when you visit the public.'

Face burning, Hannah shot back, 'I have an explanation, but obviously you have reached your own conclusion. Could you advise Mr Clarke that I'm here, please.' Hannah's tone matched that of the older woman.

As Estelle's eyes narrowed dangerously, Hannah knew that the blades had been drawn. 'Mr Clarke is at a meeting; he expected you at nine o'clock. Not one for giving a good impression, are you?' she said, again violating Hannah's attire with a scathing glance. 'Please go outside and wait at reception until he is free.' Estelle Hogg gestured dismissively.

As she left the room, Hannah fumed at the rudeness of the woman. *Not off to a good start there. What a nasty woman! I know what her Christmas present's going to be: a year's subscription of Wella Hair products.*

She briefly entertained the thought that she was being uncharitable, before indulging her whim. *Bad hair day today, Miss Hogg, or is that every day?* The thought sustained her, childishly, until the appearance of her new boss.

Paul Clarke was a tall, balding man in his thirties. He had dark good looks with an attractive Mitchumesque dimple and a hearty laugh; she liked him immediately. Paul took her hand in welcome and laughed as Hannah apologised for her late arrival and the cut of her clothes.

'Life's rarely straightforward, Hannah. Never worry,' he said, guiding her towards his office. As he came by Estelle's room, he opened the door, one hand on Hannah's elbow.

'Hold all calls, Estelle; I'll be busy with Hannah for a little while.'

Paul looked over his shoulder at Hannah. 'Have you been introduced to Estelle? I don't know what I'd do without her; she keeps me so organised that I sometimes wonder if I'm needed at all!'

'Oh, you're needed, Paul,' Estelle laughed, head tilted coquettishly.

'Yes, we've met,' nodded Hannah, amazed by the change in the older woman's demeanour.

'Oh, and by the way, Estelle, I'll need you to do Hannah's typing in the meantime – if you don't mind, that is. The other typists are very busy at present.'

'Of course,' smiled Estelle.

As Paul strode forward to his office, Hannah glanced quickly back at Estelle, who glared at her furiously. *What is her problem?* mused Hannah.

'Come in, Hannah,' Paul waved towards a chair in front of his desk. 'I'm so happy to have you join the team; it's been a while since we've had any female colleagues,' he said as he took off his jacket and placed it on the back of his chair. 'The last two ladies we had left within months of starting the job. No reflection on women, now,' he added hastily, 'just coincidence. But both cited stress for their departure. Now, I know you've had experience of the job through the voluntary sector, so I hope you'll go the distance. And don't forget that I'm always here if things get tough. You'll have a period of induction and then begin to pick up a caseload. Estelle has prioritised all the waiting cases for me, so I'll ask her to give you a file to start you off, familiarise yourself a bit with the type of problems some of our clients are facing. Any questions?'

Hannah laughed easily. 'Where do I start?' she asked.

'Yeah, I suppose that was a bit of an onslaught,' Paul laughed as he sat back in his chair.

Hannah smiled, displaying a row of even white teeth as she tumbled through a list of questions she wanted to ask. She had a natural grace about her which was striking and an eagerness in her voice that Paul found captivating, his thoughts momentarily eclipsing Hannah's words. *So young,* he thought, *was I ever like that, ever so hungry for experience?*

'I'm sorry,' said Hannah, 'I'm going on a bit.'

'Not at all, Hannah. It's good to hear some enthusiasm again. You'll find the work can sometimes be a little tough, but don't worry, you'll have plenty of support here. Come on, I'll show you to your new office.'

Paul led Hannah through to the end of the corridor. The room held three desks and two filing cabinets. It was fairly basic until you came to the window.

'That's amazing!' exclaimed Hannah. 'What a view!' The window looked out at the swollen river, which spilled and bustled over the rocky underground steps. The hills behind were etched into the sky as though copperfastened there by a celestial hand.

'So beautiful,' said Hannah. 'I'll need to have my back to this if I'm going to get any work done at all.'

Paul smiled. 'I'll send Estelle in with a file for you now so you can make a start.'

Hannah drew her hand across the MFI desk and closed her eyes. She felt a frisson of excitement. *A new start, a blank page of possibilities. She'd work hard; she'd make a difference—* Her thoughts were suddenly shattered by the thump of a red-backed file on her desk.

'The Stewart file: a difficult case,' said Estelle, 'but I'm sure you'll be fit for it,' she added, her expression enigmatic and bland, only her eyes betraying a hint of ... *what? A warning – a threat?*

***

As the weeks went by, Hannah found Paul to be a good mentor. She related well to her other male colleagues, who were always tearing in and out of the office. *Passing ships in the night.* Only at the close of each day did they have a little time to relax, and then usually only to pool thoughts about the various crises of the day. Hannah always kept up her spirits, though, and her quirky sense of humour endeared her to the rest of the staff. No matter how hard she tried to make conversation with Estelle, however, she was met with monosyllabic responses or snide remarks. 'I don't think Estelle likes me,' she told Paul during one of their supervision sessions.

'Don't take it personally,' Paul laughed. 'Estelle has had this office to herself with just us boys for some time now; she's not used to competition. She is, however, an excellent secretary; her banking background is invaluable for my budgeting responsibilities. I'd be lost without her,' he gestured to the rows of neatly marked ledgers. 'So don't worry, she'll come round in time. But if it becomes too much, let me know and I'll have a word.'

Like that's going to happen, thought Hannah wryly.

***

It was a clear day in March when Hannah was called into Paul Clarke's office. *Lord, I hope it's nothing to do with that last housing report. I had to rush it through*, she thought, unconsciously smoothing her skirt with her hands. Paul's door was closed and she knocked before entering.

'You were looking for me, Paul?' she asked, brushing her long auburn hair back from her face.

'Hannah, a second unsigned note has come into the office about the Stewart woman. It may well be malicious again, but I would like it checked out today.'

Hannah took the piece of folded foolscap paper and opened it. The words were again written with red pen and in block capitals: WHEN ARE YOU PEOPLE GOING TO DO SOMETHING ABOUT THAT GIRL AND THOSE CHILDREN? SHE'S NOT FIT TO BE A MOTHER. The name scrawled across the top was that of the young family Hannah had been allocated as her first case in this new office.

Melanie Stewart was a young widow with two children. Her husband Andrew had been killed several months earlier. The case was all the more tragic because Melanie's father-in-law, a widower and a wealthy bank manager in the town, had disapproved of his only son's marriage. It was following a heated argument over Melanie that Andrew had stormed from his father's house into the path of a speeding lorry and been killed instantly.

Hannah was reflecting on this as Paul cut in. 'Is this getting too much for you, Hannah? Estelle confided in me that she was really concerned about the reports she's been typing for you and was worried that the case might be affecting you. I've no problem reallocating this, Hannah; I'm very happy with your work to date. This is a complex case and I don't want to lose another good worker to stress.'

'No, please,' urged Hannah in a low voice. 'Please, Paul, I can handle it; I know I can.'

'Okay,' sighed Paul, 'but keep me informed. We'll be all over the headlines if anything happens to those children.'

Estelle again! Hannah gritted her teeth.

Hannah closed the door of the office behind her, unsettled by the serious allegations made against Mel Stewart, and yet still trusting her instincts that these had to be unfounded. This was the second such accusation. It was only a month ago that Hannah had to confront the young mother with the fact that someone had sent them an anonymous note to say that Mel had left her children alone.

The girl had been devastated and shocked to the core. It was clear to Hannah that the allegation was malicious. The two little girls looked healthy and happy and Mel adored them. The home was basic but clean, and she had created a warm environment for her little family, with some nice touches throughout. Hannah had tried to reassure her and of late felt that Mel was beginning to trust her and welcome her support. But now this.

Hannah bit her lip as she lifted the file again, going over all the data in case she had missed anything. She was drawn to the pen picture of Alexander Stewart.

Alexander Stewart, sixty-eight years old, widower: born in Scotland, moved to Ireland as a bank clerk where he met his future wife; moved quickly through the ranks to trainee manager, then redeployed to the city to become a respected bank manager. One son – Andrew.

Hannah noticed the word 'respected' was bracketed with pencilled inverted commas. She read on. *Personality: aloof, quiet, ambitious, austere.*

Hannah then noticed some side notes scribbled in pencil beside the main text: *intolerant, cold, bully.* She gasped! Lord, whoever wrote this profile was asking for trouble. One of the golden rules of reporting in such sensitive cases was to avoid recording personal opinion – and these were strong opinions indeed.

Poor man, she thought now, *to lose your only son … No wonder he seemed aloof.* Yet his behaviour towards Melanie after Andrew had been killed was either the act of someone deranged or calculatingly cold. *God, I'm nearly as bad*, she thought, *judging him like that*, yet it was hard to believe what he had done.

She had learned that Alexander had not attended the funeral but had chillingly sent a letter to Melanie, offering her £2,000 to hand over the children to his care.

'What kind of man is that?' Melanie had asked Hannah. 'What kind of man would want to take children from their mother?' She had spoken gently, more in disbelief than anger. When she refused his offer, Alexander had ended all contact and she had not heard from him since.

What kind of grief drives that kind of hardness and bitterness? What kind of man would refuse to contribute to his sole living bloodline, two beautiful grandchildren? Hannah could only wonder as she replaced the file in the cabinet, lifted the letter with her diary and left the office, disturbed by the thought of the task in hand.

She could feel Estelle's eyes on her as she walked to the car park. On more than one occasion, she had caught the woman watching her from the window as she went out to do her work. Well, she hadn't time to worry about her today; she needed to speak to Melanie.

Hannah approached the house, hoping she would get Mel at home. The young widow answered the door, looking as though she had the weight of the world on her shoulders.

She's paler than usual ... a little thinner, Hannah thought as she followed Mel into the living room. *The girl was twenty-four, only a year older than herself, yet seemed so much more world weary. And God knows, she had good reason.* Hannah sighed.

'The Electric people wrote to me,' said Mel, lifting the bill from the mantelpiece. 'If I don't pay the arrears, they're going to cut off the supply ... and the rent is overdue,' her voice was a monotone.

'Let me see it,' said Hannah. 'Two hundred and thirty-six pounds! That's a lot, Mel. Are you sure that's right?'

'I wouldn't know,' she said, shaking her head, 'it's just another bill. There's so many of them, I lose track.'

'Look, Mel, don't worry, we'll get them sorted. I'll go through the lot with you and we'll see what we can do.'

Hannah was aware that she had to address the issue of the allegation with Mel, but looking at the troubled face of the girl, she didn't know how to begin. She looked around the house at the spartan furniture and peeling walls. The two children were sleeping in the old-fashioned double pram by the radiator. Hannah tiptoed over and looked down into the flushed and chubby faces of the baby girls. 'They're so beautiful, Mel. You've done a good job.' Mel's eyes filled up.

Hannah reached over to pat the shoulder of the frail figure before her and with all her heart wished that she could take away some of the haunted pressure bearing down on this unhappy woman.

'Mel, this is the last thing you need to hear, but I'm afraid that there's been another allegation.' Hannah reached into her diary and brought out the letter, handing it to Mel.

Mel clutched her stomach as she read the words. 'I can't … can't …' she began, her face crumpled with anguish. Then she put down the note and walked over to her children. Whispering something to them beyond Hannah's hearing, she laid her hand on the pram.

'Mel, I know you're a good mother. Have you any idea who might be doing this?'

'It doesn't matter, really, does it?' Mel sighed. 'It's just more of the same.'

'No, you're wrong, Mel, it does matter. Get angry. Come on, you need to fight this. You deserve better. Have you any problems with your neighbours?'

'I don't know,' Melanie sighed, walking to the window. 'I've never had many dealings with them. I keep myself to myself.'

'Try not to worry, Mel. I know you're a good mother and I have no trouble standing over that anywhere.'

'Thanks, Hannah,' Mel suddenly smiled, 'thanks for everything. You've been a good support to the children and me. You know what? It doesn't matter any more; we'll be fine. You going off for your Easter holidays tomorrow?'

'Yes, tomorrow's my last day before the holiday,' Hannah replied, puzzled but pleased at the change in the young woman's mood. 'What about you? Have you any plans?'

'Oh, me and the girls will have a lovely time here. I'll take them to the park.'

'That's great, Mel. Good for you. Don't let things get you down. It can all be sorted. You're doing great.'

'Hannah, would you mind, now? I'm a wee bit tired and would like to get a bit of rest before the children wake up.'

Hannah nodded her head, 'No problem, Mel, I'll call in tomorrow. And if you need me, just ring this number. It's my direct line into the office.'

As she left, Hannah turned to wave to Mel, who had already closed the front door. Hannah suddenly felt strangely uneasy and furrowed her brow. *What's the matter?* she asked herself. *What is it?* Finding no answer, she shrugged it off and headed for her car. She had intended to return to the office for lunch before completing the rest of her scheduled visits, but it was such a beautiful day she thought she would go for a walk on the outskirts of town instead.

The day was warm and full of spring; this was her favourite time of year. Hannah stopped the car near some open ground and got out, walking the short distance to a laneway. From there, she followed the path which led to a small river, breathing deeply the clearer air and feeling some of the tension leave her body. She often came here during her lunch break. She strolled lazily, inhaling the heady scents of bramble and gorse. The morning's rain had cleared, leaving a glorious aftershock of sweetness in its wake.

Just as she approached the small car park in the clearing, she stopped suddenly. Usually empty at this time of day, Hannah was surprised to see an expensive-looking dark-blue estate car. The driver, his back to her, was gesticulating to a lady passenger. Hannah couldn't quite see her face. But she suddenly froze as she recognised the red Fiat Uno parked just behind. Just then, the driver's window glided down in one fluid motion and a creamy curl of cigarette smoke rose into the cool air.

Hannah quickly crouched down.

'I'm doing my best.' It was the faint but distinctive voice of Estelle Hogg. Hannah strained to listen. 'These things take time. How do I know you'll keep your end of the bargain?' the voice asked urgently.

'I'll have the money in your account today, but I'm not happy this is taking so long. You told me that she would break, that you could get an order against her. She's not fit to be with my grandchildren.'

'It's going the right way,' Estelle's voice held an edge. 'That new girl Carton has no experience. Lucky she came along at the right time, arrogant little madam; thinks she's doing a good job,' she laughed mirthlessly.

'I'm not interested in your petty jealousies, Estelle. I know your style, don't forget: you're quite the vicious bitch when it comes to competition. Now, I want my grandchildren – you need the money: simple business transaction. I expect you to deliver,' the driver said tersely.

Hannah's heart was now thumping in her chest as she understood the implications of the conversation. She was about to turn and run when she heard Estelle's next ominous words. 'I gave Paul another letter today, after Carton went out. I'd written that your daughter-in-law—'

'Don't call her that!' the man interrupted angrily.

'Okay,' hissed Estelle, '… that the mother was seen in the bar last night, drunk, and had left the children unattended. Paul was really alarmed. Can't take a chance with children, that's what I told him. He told me he was going to alert the police. They'll probably pick up the children until an investigation can be made into the allegations. That's when you come in and offer to keep them until the dust blows over. The girl is feeling fragile, according to Carton's reports, so it should be enough to send her over the edge. Then you're home and free.'

Hannah was stunned by what she had heard. All she could think of now was to get to the office before Estelle. Suddenly, she stopped. *Who will believe this?* she thought. *Should I confront them?* Before she could do anything, she heard car doors slam and the vehicles rev up as they exited the car park.

She had to tell Paul Clarke immediately. But something else began to tug at her thoughts – Estelle's chilling prediction: *… it should be enough to send her over the edge.* And then it struck Hannah like a hammer blow. *The way Mel had said goodbye, the brightness of her eyes. Melanie – she had to get to Melanie.* Hannah ran back to her car and drove straight to Melanie's home.

Hannah's heart was racing. The curtains were drawn. She knocked loudly on the door, but no-one answered. Hannah hurried to the back of the house and was met with a similar scene. She tried to see through the curtains, pulled tight at the back of the house, to no avail. Knocking frantically at the windows, Hannah began to shout, 'Mel, Mel, are you there? Let me in!' There was still no reply so she banged at the back door and then pushed at it. The lock was faulty and, after another hard push, it burst open.

The stillness of the house was the first thing she noticed. Hannah called out as she went into the hall. 'Mel, where are you?' Hannah moved quickly now. *She must be out*, she thought, *must be out; there's nobody here.* In the kitchen, she looked around. Two unwashed cups lay on the worktop beside the kettle. The box containing the baby's feed lay open, powdered milk scattered around. A smaller brown pill bottle lay on its side, the grainy residue of its contents coating a nearby spoon. Hannah grabbed the bottle; the yellow dust of the Valium was all that remained in the bottle and she could feel bile beginning to rise in her throat as she forced herself now to the bedroom.

Mel lay on top of the bed, her arms around each of her babies. Hannah raced over to them. Melanie was still breathing. She put her finger to the neck pulse of each of the children; there was the tiniest fluttering, but only just. Grabbing her mobile phone, Hannah dialled 999, her hands shaking so much she thought she might drop it.

'Emergency! Emergency!' she screamed to the operator, giving the address and shouting it was a matter of life or death.

Now she lifted the youngest child, breathing into her mouth, willing her to stay, shouting at Melanie, shaking the other child.

Ambulances wailed in the distance, ever nearer as Hannah fought with all the strength she could muster to hold on.

Jesus, Lord God, help me. Help them, she prayed.

'Melanie! Melanie!' she shouted. 'Hold on! Hold on!'

***

Later, at the hospital, Hannah pressed her head against the glass window of the children's unit. The two girls lay side-by-side, pink cheeks flushed in their butterfly-white cots. Melanie, her head back, was asleep on the chair, her hand through the bars of the nearest cot, clutching the tiny fingers of her younger child. Her face was relaxed and serene.

Hannah felt a single tear roll down her cheek. In these last short months she had been faced with the real world. She had witnessed the vagaries of the human spirit, both good and bad. She shivered, remembering the look in Estelle's eyes as she turned slowly towards Hannah before the police car drove her away. Hannah's carefree days were gone. *Could she cope with this responsibility? Was she really cut out for this?*

She closed her eyes as tiredness overwhelmed her. She knew only one thing: if the young mother before her had the courage to go on, then she would be there for her. Their journeys were now inextricably linked.

As Hannah turned to leave, she looked through the window one final time to find Melanie awake and smiling up at her.

FOOTSTEPS

Michael's eyes snapped open. His heart was hammering in his chest, his shoulders and neck slick with sweat. He breathed deeply before reaching for the clock on his bedside table. Five thirty, it read.

Another restless night almost over, each toss and turn a tick of the second hand, a torturous, sleepless revolution of the hours. Time was holding on to him, each slippery minute a bonus, a triumph of matter over mind.

On the rare occasions he dozed, he woke on the half-hour. *Was he born on the half-hour? Same as Anna?* He knew exactly when *she* was born: thirty minutes past six. He knew because it was on the morning of his tenth birthday. He could still hear his father.

'Happy birthday, Michael, do you want to see your present?'

And there she was, in his mother's arms, the tiniest little thing, all eyes in a clean, white head.

'Your baby sister,' whispered his father, his voice soft like cotton wool.

'She's mine?'

'All yours, sweetheart,' said his mother.

'And a fort, with cowboys and Indians,' added his father quickly.

'What will I call her?'

'Anna,' said his mother.

'Anna …' he'd said, counting all her little fingers and toes. 'Can I keep her?'

***

38

Michael punched his fist hard into the pillow now, but it was no good; Anna's mottled face was still there. She moved through his days and haunted his nights. He pressed the palms of his hands tightly together and then opened them like a book. These were the hands which once carried her tiny schoolbag, guided her pencil, mussed her hair. These were the hands which rushed to swing her high on his holidays home, the same hands which, one year ago today, traced the red and angry rope burns on her cold and coffined slender neck.

God, how much longer till daybreak? And then what? Would that be any better? Would he get any ease? He threw the switch above his head and pulled himself up onto the pillow, dragging his tired grey eyes around the room. The walls were hessian hung and peeling. Empty whiskey bottles were balanced precariously against the wall. His clothes were strewn side by side with his carpentry tools, which were a nod to a token occupation and a means to an end. The only redeeming feature in the room was an original 1900s fireplace, lined with dark green and yellow tiles, which was burnished a bit from heat but cold and empty now and blocked by a crude piece of Formica.

He had no desire to change anything; in this room or in his life; he was in transition.

Not far away, he heard again the familiar sound of a door closing and the clatter of a woman's heels hurrying past his window. He checked the time again. Almost quarter to six. *She's late*, he thought. When he first moved here, her steps were just an added torture but they slowly rooted into his day, a welcome distraction to the bleakness of his thoughts. He knew exactly how many footsteps she took from her front door to the point beyond his hearing and back again. The seasons saw a change in their rhythm, from the lightness in the long days to the uncertain over-the-shoulderness of dark mornings like today. He no longer wondered where she was going. The facts were established: she had to be somewhere for six o'clock, where she stayed for one hour or thereabouts before returning home.

He looked forward to her steps now; they brought a promise of something, he wasn't sure what. But the regular rhythm of her dawn walk comforted him in a way he didn't need to understand.

He imagined what she might look like. She was young, that much he discerned from those days she passed a little late. *How could she run in those things?* For they were certainly high heels, the click-clip of them smarting the pavement, charting her path.

One morning she stumbled, just outside his window. He imagined the double take and almost heard the gasp as she steadied herself. As she walked on, he could hear that the click-clip had changed to a staccato de-dum and guessed that she must have gone over on her ankle.

In his head, he rushed to help her, put a gentle arm around her and soothe her, but the blurred deadness of his will washed the thought away.

As her footsteps faded now in the distance, Michael rose and dressed quickly. He could set his clock by her, though that would be superfluous, given his erratic sleep pattern. Two hours of whiskey-induced stupor and a bedful of restless circling till dawn was his lot.

He tried to remember the last time he felt rest, easement. A powerful memory returned.

***

He is nineteen years old; soft footsteps move impatiently outside his room in St Patrick's College, the seminary in Maynooth, not far from Dublin.

'Michael, are you coming? It's nearly midnight. Come on!'

'You go first, Andy.'

Andy shakes his head and runs a hand through his tousled jet black hair in mock amazement. 'Michael Connors, I'm shocked. Don't tell me you're scared?' he teases.

'Terrified,' confesses Michael, though he has a trick up his sleeve for Andy.

'Some priest you're going to make, Michael, if you're scared by a stupid story. Come on, cowardy,' he whispers, leading the way. As they pass through the quiet corridors, Michael catches his reflection in the window. His lean body is crouched forward like an athlete about to sprint. The look in his eyes is of anticipation, exhilaration, and his mouth has the slice of a smile, which widens as they approach their destination.

Now they're standing outside the famous ghost room. Andy puts his eye to the keyhole just as Michael glides a bird's feather over the back of his friend's neck, unprepared for the scream. Fast footsteps then as they fly to the safety of their bedrooms, tumbling down and laughing, and peace.

***

Yes, peace then, innocence and peace lying in his own bed in St Pat's, arms above his head, window wide open to the vast black cap of night and the stars full of His promise. A surge of supreme wellbeing, the certainty that all is well, and peace – waves and waves of it warming his spirit, slipping him into the most restful sleep he has ever known, or is ever likely to know again.

He realised he was crying now and fiercely wiped away the tears. From the photograph on his bedside table, Anna's innocent, smiling eyes followed his every move. He picked up the picture, held it to his chest for a brief moment, then turned it face down.

Anna, ballerina Anna, light as fairy dust. He saw her then; five years old and walking beside him from school.

***

'Michael, you'll have to carry my schoolbag. I have to think,' sighing deeply.

'Okay, little grub, hand it over. Must be very important.'

'What?' she looks up at him.

'What you're thinking.'

'I'm thinking what I'll be when I grow up.'

'And what are you going to be?'

'A famous ballerina and a beautiful lady.' She turns her little head from him in a gesture of mini-hauteur as he laughs. 'What's funny?' she asks in a tight little voice.

'Nothing at all. I think that's great. Do you know what I'm going to be?'

'What?' She stops walking, giving him her full attention.

'A priest.'

'A priest, Michael?' Her cornflower blue eyes are wide with interest. 'That's the best job in the whole world.'

'And why's that?' he asks, smiling at her earnest little face.

'Because you get to talk in the chapel.'

'Oh, is that so?' he says. 'And why do little children have to be quiet in the chapel?'

'Because all the people are sleeping, of course.'

Michael bursts out laughing. 'Go on, I'll race ye home,' he says.

And she runs ahead of him, her golden, baby-breath hair flying in the breeze as she turns to shout to him, 'Bye, Michael. Love you.'

'You, too,' he says.

***

The yellow sun in his chest now darkened as her image dissolved and was replaced by powder-coated sweet tones – the hateful voice of corruption.

'Mrs Connors, can I borrow Anna again after school this afternoon? I need some of my files sorted before the inspection. I'll make sure she goes straight home afterwards.'

'Certainly, Father.'

He squeezed his eyes tight shut against the pain – *God, if only I'd been there* – snapping them open as his mother's voice calls him back again.

'Michael, have a word with Anna, will you? She's refusing to go to school and won't listen to me or your dad. She'll listen to you.'

'Sorry, Mam, I have to go. I'm covering the Retreat tonight. Tell Anna I'll give her a ring tomorrow. And don't be worrying so much, she's fourteen, hormones flying; it's probably about a boy.'

***

He is in his room in the parochial house when his friend Father John comes in. John's immense frame usually fills the room but today he looks oddly diminished.

'Michael, you have to go home. There's been an accident.'

'Accident? What's happened?' *His mother? His father?*

'It's your sister, Michael. I'm so very sorry.' John's gentle voice catches and he reaches forward as Michael backs away.

'My sister? Anna? No, that couldn't be, John. I spoke to Mam only last night; she didn't say anything. What kind of accident?'

'Michael, you need to go home now.' John can no longer look in his eyes.

'What kind of accident, John?' he repeats, though he knows.

***

'Michael, she left you a note.' His mother and father sit beside each other.

Michael, I'm so sorry. I'm so sorry for all this hurt; I'm a very bad person ...

It was his mother who guessed, who told him, grief fragmenting the few words which were needed.

His devastation and anger were unappeased by the pale grey response from the parish administrator. 'I'm so sorry, Michael, we can't tell you where, but I can tell you that he's been sent away to an enclosed order.'

All the sad embarrassment of his colleagues and the long, anguished talks with Andy and John were not enough. He couldn't stay; his centre had broken.

'The Message is still the same, Michael,' his mother gently wept as he held his parents close for the longest time before leaving his home and his faith for distant shores.

***

Michael walked slowly to the kitchen. Sweating heavily, he reached for the kettle and the whiskey bottle. Outside, a grey mist like a silk stocking rolled slowly down towards morning. Inexplicably, the twitter and screech of wheeling birds fanned a distant flame. Birdsong, his mother's favourite sound, and from somewhere nearby, the scent of turf, her favourite fragrance – the power of the memory jolted him.

He checked the time, almost seven, and absently he waited for the return of his unknown friend. In a moment of strange alignment, just as the kettle began to whistle, Michael heard a cry from the street. He lifted the kettle from the gas and stood stock-still. Again he heard the sound, though he couldn't be sure from where.

With mounting anxiety, he quickly pulled on his jacket and dashed out into the cold of the day. The street was deserted. He ran towards the old railway line, looking into side streets as he passed. All was silent.

He stopped and listened again. Nothing. He began to doubt himself. *Maybe the lack of sleep*, he thought. But no, he was wide awake, his senses on alert; he could almost feel his ears raised like antennae.

He walked slowly on now, peering into derelict buildings and darkened laneways. The chill of the morning air began to seep into his skin and he wrapped his arms around himself. He was just about to give up when he thought he heard a muffled sound coming from an alleyway across the street.

Cautiously, he made his way over, peering into it, the hairs on the back of his neck rising. He wasn't sure but he thought he could make out a dark figure bending over. Then, suddenly, the definite sound of a woman's voice. 'Help me!' a strangled scream.

He was frightened. Never a great soldier, he hesitated before calling out, 'Hey, you!' hoping to scare away the attacker.

No answer. He moved slightly forward and as he did, the figure turned and charged at him, knocking him backwards. Michael saw the glint of the knife before he felt the blade enter his side.

Behind him in the alleyway, he heard the woman sobbing as she slowly approached, her pace quickening when she saw him on the ground. 'Oh, my God, you're hurt!' she cried, looking down at the dark red slick which was coating his hand. 'I'll get help. Don't move!' And then she was running in her bare feet, banging at doors and shouting for help, calling for an ambulance before rushing back to his side. She carried her heels in one hand and her knees were bleeding and cut through the torn nylon.

'Did he hurt you?' his voice came haltingly in mini-breaths.

'If you hadn't come …' her voice emptied itself into the cold of the dawn as though her life itself had drained away. She shivered. 'I thought I was going to die; I didn't think anyone would hear.'

'I was waiting for your footsteps back,' he struggled to stay awake. 'I hear you going past my door every morning.'

'What's your name?' she asked him, willing him to stay with her.

'Michael,' he said, feeling himself drift into a peace he hadn't known for a long time.

'Stay with me, Michael, stay awake. Help's coming.' She reached up and undid the scarf at her neck and pressed it firmly to his side.

He opened his eyes as her long hair brushed his cheek. It curled softly back from her temples, framing anxious eyes the colour of an autumn leaf. She reminded him a little of Anna, of how Anna might have grown.

'Where do you go all these mornings?' his voice seemed far away from him.

'Mass,' she said simply, as though it were the most natural thing in the world. *Keep talking to him*, she thought, *keep him awake*. 'You know, Michael, they say when you save a life, you're responsible for it for the rest of your own life. So don't you think of going anywhere. Just hang on. Help's nearly here.'

'Mass,' he struggled to keep his eyes on hers.

'I know,' she shrugged slightly, a faint smile working at her mouth, 'it's a faith thing.'

And from a distant home shore, he heard the echo of parting words: *the Message is still the same, Michael.*

The girl reached down and cradled his head into her lap. 'You're going to make it, Michael. Stay with me.'

'Yes,' he said.

He closed his eyes.

Anna was sitting on the kerbside beside him, her arms hugging her knees as she turned round to look at him, smiling. Her face was radiant, her eyes shining. After a few reassuring seconds, her ghostwhite lips mouthed the words, 'Bye, Michael. Love you,'

'You, too,' he murmured.

In the near distance, the sound of the sirens grew ever closer and with them, he realised, the promise of a new beginning.

THE NEGATIVE PHOTOGRAPHER

Henry was out of sorts, which was a bit of a pity because his day had begun well. His phone had gone off at seven as he lay snuggled beneath his *Star Trek* duvet cover.

Could he do a great favour and cover a wedding? asked a friend who'd had to cancel at the last minute. Well, he wasn't actually a friend, more an acquaintance through the paper. He'd agreed far too quickly, didn't even ask why the guy had to cancel. He should have made him sweat a little, not appeared so desperate; still, it was done now and truth be told, he was looking forward to it.

It had been a while since he'd been asked to do a wedding. He mostly covered parties and pub nights now, taking photographs of legless, half-naked teenagers, all loved up with their 'best friends'. What was wrong with their parents? If he'd been their father, he'd have thrashed them within an inch of their lives. Mind you, that was nothing compared to the chaotic children's 'fun days'. It was all he could do at times to stop himself slapping some of them sideways, what with their screaming, pulling at him and giving him the fingers. He had to be careful, though: some uppity, overprotective mother had made a complaint after he had made her son cry. He'd done nothing, really, just told the child he'd vaporise him with his laser if he didn't stop bumping into him. It was a joke, for God's sake! Had they no sense of humour? But yes, he promised the boss he would be professional at all times from now on.

It would be good to work with civilised people for a change. He gathered up his equipment, grabbing his lucky

48

Captain Kirk figure at the last minute and set off in his battered car.

Henry was fairly flying down the road, tapping his fingers on the wheel to the beat from the car radio, when three fat pheasants chose that particular moment to take their morning stroll. The poor creatures instead took their last involuntary flights, propelled by the bumper of Henry's car high into the air amidst an explosion of feathers. Slamming on the brakes, he skidded to the side of the road, bouncing off the kerb before screeching to a halt. Henry jumped out of the car, cursing at the sight of the burst tyre. 'What is the bloody point of having wings if you decide to walk everywhere?' he roared in frustration at the dead birds.

Later at the garage, he'd banged his head on the tyre of a suspended car and landed with a thump on the ground, his head buzzing. He reminded himself to give 'lucky' Captain Kirk a good hiding later on.

And so it was in this mounting bad form that Henry arrived at the job. And it didn't improve. The mother of the bride could talk for Ireland. She had given him at least forty instructions since he'd arrived at the house. Now she was over at the bridesmaids, tweaking this and that and bending down to even out the hems of their dresses.

She was a large lady with the biggest rear end Henry had ever seen. *Lord bless us*, he thought, *you could mount a piano on it*.

'Well, are you going to take pictures or just stand there gawping?' she said, turning to him, an unpleasant expression on her face as though she'd read his thoughts.

'Okay,' said Henry. *She's got the nerve of Nelson*, he thought. 'Right, line up. Mum, could you—'

'I hate that,' called the mother.

'Pardon?' said Henry.

'The "mum" thing; hate it,' she said. 'It's Mrs Scott. Now,

would you ever get a move on? We're never going to get to the church.'

Henry was stung. He closed his eyes, picturing himself jumping up and down on her face, then opened them and smiled. 'Okay, let's get yourself sorted here, Mrs Scott, and you can go on.' He held up the digital camera, trying to get the most flattering angle. 'Just a little to the right … that's it. Okay, let's try some casual shots now. Walk towards me a little … yes, that's right … no, just a little,' he warned as his lens began to fill alarmingly. 'Right, okay, stop. Now, turn around and look back over your shoulder at me as though you'd forgotten something.'

Big mistake! Not only did it take ten minutes to bring her round after the fall, but the feather thing on her head stabbed him in the eye as he reached forward to steady her, nearly blinding him. And she had the nerve to blame him! He had to close his ears against the rant and think of something pleasant – like space, the final frontier.

He was beginning to understand why his 'buddy' had passed on this one. Take the father of the bride: think falling off the ugly tree and hitting every branch on the way down.

Oh, Henry knew he was no oil painting himself – he'd kept the same face since he was fifteen, even though everything else about him had carried on regardless. His mother had assured him that he was special; she wasn't joking. He was a fifty-year-old man in a boy's face. That could have done for him if he hadn't made an effort. But he did the business – put on the glasses, slicked back the hair, became a sort of freaky Cliff Richard lookalike. And he dressed well, an attribute noticeably missing from the poor man who was now pushing his wife, with difficulty, through the doors of the first wedding car. The unfortunate husband was wearing a pale-blue suit with a yellow shirt, blue and red tie and blue espadrilles. *Where did he think he was – in Hawaii? It was warm, granted, but he was in the middle of bloody Donegal, for God's sake!* He was also suspiciously bright eyed; Henry reckoned he might have a little nip in him.

'Hey, mister,' a cheeky voice interrupted his train of thought.

From the cut of him, Henry deduced he was one of the family. 'You talking to me?'

'Aye, me ma says you're useless.'

'Is that right?' said Henry, trying desperately to think of an adult response. 'Well, your ma's got an arse the size of the *Titanic*. Now, get lost.'

Henry didn't move quickly enough to avoid the hefty kick the little monster landed squarely on his shin. 'You're dead,' he muttered, rubbing his leg.

'Leon,' shouted the father, 'get in the car with your mother! Now!' The boy gestured a two-fingered salute before scuttling away.

'Leon … hmm,' Henry murmured as he narrowed his eyes. 'Okay, Leon, game on.'

With the nightmare of mother and son departed, Henry had time to consider the bride. *Please, God, let her belong to a different gene pool*, he thought, just as the words of the old Spike Jones hilarious parody played out in his head: *I went to your wedding, although I was dreading, the thought of seeing you. Your mother was crying, your father was crying, and I was crying, too.*

He felt a bubble of giddiness in his throat; it was one of his favourite records. 'Control yourself, Henry, you're a professional,' he said aloud.

He concentrated on snapping the bridesmaids. Were they her sisters? He hadn't got round to asking them. He hoped not. The smaller of the two had to have a thyroid problem – that could be the only explanation for the bulging eyes.

As for Miss Eiffel Tower, what did they think he was – a magician? He would worry about the group shots later, but in the meantime he managed to achieve a balance of sorts by sitting them both in the car and avoiding profiles.

He was setting up now for the bride when the distinctive clip-clop and snort of horses stopped him dead. And there it was: he should have guessed. Yes, it was going to be one of those days. Not satisfied with giving him concussion this morning, God was on a roll. He wondered if this was some kind of celestial *Candid Camera* scene from that great Old Kidder in the sky.

Oh, the horses were lovely, if you liked horses. But try cantering beside them, your camera strap tangled in their reins, and it's a whole different bag of balls. Yes, that had happened to him. He thought he'd been sent for, and the worst of it was the street kids who followed him down the road, boisterous with laughter and shooting the whole thing on their mobile phones. The bride had gone ballistic and refused to pay for the pictures when she realised she was part of the subsequent *YouTube* clip entitled *Runaway Bride*. He had probably come across with one expletive too many when she confronted him; after all, he was the one who'd been laid up for a week with severe groin strain.

That had been another unwarranted complaint.

'That's all people think about these days,' he'd said to the boss, 'complaints, complaints.' Easy way out, if you'd asked him. The boss didn't ask him and he hadn't done a wedding since.

He waited with double trepidation now, ready to capture the moment of the bride's appearance on the steps. The neighbours had gathered in little pockets around the house, smoking and chatting. *All good*, thought Henry, *all good – nobody was laughing.*

And then she emerged.

Well the figure wasn't too bad, if you looked past the face. She either had serious liver disease or the tanning rooms had exploded with her in them. The dress was decent enough, but he thought she should lose the white umbrella. Not easy to juggle flowers, umbrella, and dad's arm, unless you were on *Crackerjack*. He'd have a word at the church. 'Good,' he called. 'Right. Where's Dad?'

And on cue, *Miami Vice* sailed through the door like he was on coasters. His face was so red it looked like he'd put it on inside out. *Definitely on the juice*, thought Henry.

'Whoops,' said the father, 'ready.'

'Okay, Bride …' *What was her name?* He reached into his pocket and brought out the card: Cillya Scott. C-I-L-L-Y-A. He spelled it out. *Unusual name.* 'Cilla?'

'No, it's pronounced Celia, like, after David McCallum.'

'David McCallum?'

'You know, Illya Kuryakin.'

'Her mother's a total *Man from U.N.C.L.E.* freak,' explained her dad, which came out something like 'hermaaassmanfrmunclefrik'.

'Me ma's a big *Man from U.N.C.L.E.* fan. Think me and April were the lucky ones,' said Cillya as though the father hadn't spoken. 'The boys didn't get off so lightly.'

Henry concluded from this exchange that the father of the bride was invisible or Cillya was deaf.

'Oh, right. Well, each to their own,' said Henry, thinking, *well, I'm a Trekkie myself but I don't think I'd have called any of my children Uhura or Spock. The mother should be locked up.*

'Okay, troops, let's get this show on the road. Right, Cillya, just hold it there … lovely … that's it. Now, just lower the flowers a little … no, a little more … that's it … down from your face … good. Now, Dad, lean in a little so it doesn't look like you have the Panama Canal between you. On second thoughts, Cillya, maybe you could move over … that's it.

Now, take your dad's arm … good. Right, that's a wrap. Let's get you to the chapel.'

Henry gathered up his equipment and moved quickly down to the road.

The carriage drivers looked impressive, he had to admit, top hats and tails, but the horses … *Well,* he thought, *why am I surprised?* The horses were wearing little veils over their blinkers, and the manes and tails were plaited with white-and-yellow ribbons, with a horseshoe attached to the bottom end of each one. *Mental note, contact the USPCA later.* He was careful to keep a good distance from the creatures; there would be no repeat of his impression of Trigger.

When they had all assembled at the church, Henry resumed the task of adjusting and managing the shape and size dynamic of the wedding party. *Dear God*, he thought, mopping his brow, *if there was ever the need for a saint for hopeless wedding cases, it was now.*

The day will soon be over, though, he told himself, and then he was going to take up fishing – anything but photography. Thank God the mother had gone inside with the boy; the bruise on his shin stinging like mad reminded him that he still owed the little creep. *Careful, Henry*, he thought, *remember what the boss had said on that last occasion*: 'You have a responsibility, Henry, to the community. Do your job, ignore personalities, be professional and sensible, then just leave. I don't want any more complaints.'

Yes, he was dead right. *Get on with it*, thought Henry, wishing he could up sticks and leave this one right now; it was like a penance.

And what the hell was that awful smell? As if in answer to his question, a loud whinny of satisfaction rang through the air. Henry followed the aroma to the bridal carriage where the high tail of the leading horse signposted the hot deposit on the ground. 'Oh, for heaven's sake!' screeched the bride.

'Get those horses out of there. Take them round the block and get that cleaned up. Now!'

Henry was dying to laugh, but the look on the bride's orange face drew him up short.

He coughed loudly before continuing. 'Right, then, Cillya, just stand there.' He moved Cillya behind him, stapled to her father, who had sobered up a little and was standing as though he had the church spire up his behind.

The organ music had begun and the doors to the church were opened. Henry turned around, waiting for the priest to come onto the altar, only to find the demonic figure of his adversary grinning at him. 'Hey, Useless!' taunted the sneering face.

'Napoleon, get back inside,' whispered the bride loudly.

'Napoleon?' said Henry.

'Leon,' corrected the girl quickly.

'So, it's Napoleon, is it?' said Henry quietly, his day suddenly looking a whole lot better.

'Shut up, you. It's Leon. Only me ma's allowed to call me that.'

'Whatever, Napoleon,' he said, unable to resist descending to the boy's level.

'Shut up!' hissed Leon, clenching his fists.

'Oh, I'm so scared,' said Henry, wiggling his free hand in the air, all thoughts of the boss gone from his head.

That was all the encouragement Leon needed as he put down his head and charged.

'Leon!' screamed the bride as Henry deftly sidestepped and the boy ended up inside his sister's veil.

As the brat propelled himself onward, trying to escape, the veil became a kite, billowing out and launching Cillya and her attached father backwards, teetering precariously before landing right slap-bang in the middle of the steaming pile recently deposited by the relieved horse.

In the ominous silence that followed, Henry debated whether he should offer a hand up or run. There was no doubt that Napoleon was in for a hammering. *Account closed*, he thought, brushing off his hands.

But before he had time to do anything, he felt the hot breath of the boy's mother on his neck. Leon was up on his feet, shouting and pointing, 'It was all his fault, Ma; he said you had a big arse!'

'That's it. I knew you were useless,' said the furious Mrs Scott. 'You're that eejit that ended up tangled in the horses, aren't you? I should have known you'd be a disaster, you moron. Well, I can tell you now, you'll never work in this town again.'

Henry thought that last bit was uncalled for and wanted to tell Mrs Scott this in his most professional manner. He made way for her now as she pushed past him, bending down to assist her daughter. A terrible mistake!

Henry accepted he didn't really have any choice. Fate was beckoning and it could not be denied; the proximity of the offending huge behind was simply a frontier too far. So he planted a well-aimed boot smack in the middle before taking to his heels.

***

Later, as he lay in his bed, he felt a great sense of freedom. His photography days were over. He would boldly go into the unknown, face new challenges, explore uncharted territory. *The day had ended well after all*, he thought as he took Captain Kirk down from the shelf.

'Beam me up, Scottie,' he said with a smile, drawing up his covers and switching off the light.

HOMECOMING

Nora gently took her mother's arm as she stumbled. 'Just hold on to me, Mother. It'll be all right,' she said.

Maeve smiled at her daughter gratefully before bending again into the chill Atlantic wind. The graveyard in Aranmore was empty as they threaded their way through the grey granite and black marble, stopping now and then as Maeve recognised an old neighbour or friend now gone. Then they were there. Nora let go her mother's arm as Maeve moved forward tentatively to the grave of her own beloved parents. 'I'm home,' she whispered. 'I've come home.'

Nora was overwhelmed with a kaleidoscope of emotion. *It's over,* she thought, *and yet it has only begun.* She turned to the dark, brooding waters below as she was transported back to that morning only a few months before but which seemed like an age ago now, when hope and despair had fused, creating a destiny she had never imagined.

***

Nora Magill had risen early and pulled a robe around her slender arms before going downstairs to draw the curtains and light the fire. She was eighteen years old. A mane of copper-coloured curls, which she hastily pinned back now, framed an intelligent face.

The fire lit, Nora called to her grandfather and began making breakfast. John Magill followed her wearily into the kitchen. His bony frame scaffolded a spotless simmit. Worn leather braces held up his sagging trousers and a pale-blue shirt, the colour of his eyes, lay tipsily over his arm. Nora smiled as she turned to greet him. 'Morning, Granda. How are you feeling this morning?'

Before John could answer, he was overcome by a wracking cough, harsh and guttural. As the spasms continued, John held on to the side of the table, motioning for a glass of water. When at last the cough subsided, he sat down heavily on the worn leather chair by the fire. Struggling to find his breath, he turned to Nora, wiping his brow, 'I'm feeling a bit tired today, love, and I think I'll not bother with breakfast.'

Nora busied herself around the kitchen, frowning to herself as she felt a vague anxiety steal over her. Her grandfather was all she had in this world. His cough was not going away, and despite medication, he was not getting any better. He had been growing more distant recently, staring out at the ocean, wearing a look of unbearable sadness. She worried about him but felt powerless to help him in these days.

She moved over now to where he sat, his gnarled hand trembling as he held it over the heat. 'What's the matter, Granda, do you not feel well?' she asked as she hunkered down before him.

John looked down at his beloved granddaughter. 'I dreamt of your grandmother last night, Nora. She was dancing and laughing. She wanted me to dance as well and we turned and twirled, spinning wildly across the floor. All our old friends were there. I didn't want to wake up.' John sighed deeply as he turned his head towards the door. 'Nora,' he said softly as to himself, 'Nora, Nora …'

'What is it, Granda?' Nora reached over and took his hands in hers, stroking them gently, acutely aware of how cold they were. 'Tell me what's the matter.'

Her grandfather sighed and with dimmed rheumy eyes indicated to the cupboard above the range. 'Do you see the black box up there, Nora? Bring it down to me.'

Nora reached up to the top of the press, puzzled by the despair in his voice. 'Is this it, Granda?' she asked, stumbling a little as her foot caught on the side of the fender.

John lifted the box, all the while his hand trembling, and held it. Then, withdrawing a key from his trouser pocket, he turned it in the lock. 'Nora, listen to me now. I told you that your mother, our Maeve, died in England shortly after you were born, but that wasn't the true story.' Nora sat down on her chair; she became very still. John kept his eyes on the box. 'God, Nora, I'm so sorry. I should have told you years ago.' He dragged a hand through his hair.

'Go on, Granda.' Nora wanted to run from the room, such was the surge of anxiety she felt.

'Your mother was as beautiful as you are now, but twice as wild. She hated the island; she called it Alcatraz and was always running to the mainland any chance she'd get.' John sighed deeply. 'We worried about her, of course, but she was very headstrong. Anyway, one day out of the blue, she left us a note saying she was off to England to find work. Your grandmother was shattered; I don't think she ever really recovered. Maeve sent us a few postcards, but it was nearly a year before she returned.'

Nora kept her eyes on the tin box, waiting, as John continued.

'She arrived home one day, unexpectedly, and you were in her arms.' John broke down quite suddenly. 'We were so happy to see her,' his voice was weak and broken with tears. 'We knew then why she had gone, and we let her know all we wanted was her happiness, but she was very quiet; she didn't look well,' he said, wiping his eyes.

'"*Will you take care of her for me?*" Those were her words. "*I can't stay here. It's the judgement: I could see it in their eyes as soon as I came off the ferry. They'll never let it go.*" I pleaded with her to stay, but she had made up her mind. She could hardly look at us as she said she would come back for you when she was settled. But we never saw her again.'

'So did she die there, Granda? Do you know?' Nora's voice became more urgent.

John bowed his head. 'No, child, she didn't. But your grandmother passed away just over a year later … when you were barely two years old; Maeve had broken her heart. I know she never got over losing her only child, and while you were a blessing, Nora, the grief was just too much for her. Years went by and I heard nothing from Maeve. Then this letter arrived when you were about ten. I couldn't give it to you: I was so angry with Maeve, Nora, so angry …'

John's voice broke off, thick with emotion. And then, with a trembling hand, he reached into the box and withdrew a letter and a simple solid silver cross, both of which he handed to Nora.

My little Nora, this is a hard letter to write. You are ten years old already. I left you when you were very young because I was in a very bad place then, and have been for a long time. You needed love and stability and I knew you'd be safe and happy with your grandparents, so I took you back home from England. I had hurt my father and mother so much already, but even then, I couldn't stay. I was a coward, but I knew that you would be happy on Aranmore until I could get on my feet. It's been a long journey, Nora. I was so unhappy in England, but too proud to write and ask to come home. I've been in America now for two years, Nora, and finally have a job and am feeling good for the first time in years. I miss you so much. I'm coming home in the autumn. I've nearly saved the fare. I want to see you, see my mother and father, tell them I'm sorry and thank them. Oh, Nora, I can't wait to see you. I'm

sending you a silver cross I got at the Mission out here;
I want you to wear it until I see you again.

All my love,
Your mother,
Maeve.

Nora took her grandfather's hands as the old man's eyes
filled with tears that flowed unchecked down his cheeks. 'I
wrote back to Maeve, Nora. I told her that her mother was
dead, had died because *she* broke her heart, told her I didn't
want to see her. She didn't come in the autumn; she sent two
more letters and I sent them back unopened. Later, as you
grew up so like your mother, I realised how wrong I was and
wrote to Maeve, asking her to come home, telling her I was
sorry. The letter returned, marked *not at this address*. Nora,
I'm so sorry. Nothing I can say or do will ever make up for
what I did. I've been a bitter old man.'

Nora stood up and went to the piano where a picture of
her mother sat. She stared at the young woman in the frame.
Maeve had turned to the camera just as someone called her,
a look of surprise widening her extraordinary green eyes; her
hair was haloed by golden sunlight, one blending seamlessly
with the other. She was wearing a simple white sleeveless
dress, her right shoulder raised flirtatiously to her chin as she
dangled her straw bonnet by her side. Nora stood rooted,
unable to take it in: *she was alive … her mother was alive*.
Her thoughts were interrupted as her grandfather came over
to her.

John was agitated and restless, fumbling with the cross
and chain. 'I want you to wear this cross, Nora. Put it on, it's
your connection to Maeve. It will bring you to her. Wear it
for me, love.'

Nora's mind was in turmoil as she placed the chain

around her neck. Her grandfather was now pacing back and forward, running his hand through his hair, over and over. 'Shush, Granda, don't worry. It's all right. Come on, lie down now and I'll bring you a cup of tea. Look, I'm wearing the cross. You have a rest and we'll work out what to do later.'

Calmness seemed to settle over John then as he allowed Nora to lead him to the old moquette sofa in the corner, where he soon lapsed into a restless sleep. Nora went back to the fire, stoking the embers before putting more turf on the top. The acrid but fragrant aroma permeated the room and Nora was suddenly touched with a frisson of fear and foreboding. *Her mother was alive all these years.* She shivered involuntarily; *why was he telling her this now?*

Her thoughts were suddenly broken by the onset of an alarming sound from John. A deep and rasping noise, as though he was drowning, spurred Nora quickly to his side. 'Do you want a drink of water, Granda?' she asked, alarmed by his pallor and the blue tinges around his lips. John was unable to speak as his gasps became more laboured and collided with the spasms shuddering through his body. He was holding on to Nora now, panic beginning to rise.

'I'll get the doctor, Granda. I'll not be long.' Nora leapt to her feet, running to the door and onto the narrow road. 'Rose! Rose!' she shouted to her neighbour. 'Get the doctor; get the priest! Something's wrong with my grandfather.'

She raced back to the house and to her grandfather. John was quite still. Nora knew that he had gone. She sank to her knees, shocked to the core. *Had he known?* she wondered.

She stayed by his side long after the doctor, the priest and the 'waking' neighbours had gone. She knew what she had to do. Bending close beside his head, Nora kissed his brow and whispered to him, 'I'll find her, Granda. I'll find her and bring her home.'

***

When the plane came in to land at New York's Kennedy Airport, Nora realised she was unconsciously pulling at the silver cross on her neck. Her grandfather's words echoed in her mind: *this is your connection to Maeve; it will bring you to her.* She had booked a flight almost immediately after his funeral, the feeling of lost time almost overwhelming.

As she deplaned, Nora held the letter bearing the only address she had for her mother in tight, trembling hands. She prayed quietly to her grandfather to guide her now as she ventured forward, her resolve and purpose undiminished by the massive task she faced.

'What's the address again, lady?' the cab driver asked as he eyed her through his rear mirror.

'Block Sixty-Four, West Fifty-Fifth Street, Queens.' Nora sat forward in her seat. 'Is it far?'

The cab driver shrugged, 'Be there in about twenty.'

The front of the building was run down, broken windows jutting through like bits of shattered bone. The street was deserted as Nora stepped down from the cab. 'Would you mind waiting?' she asked the driver nervously. 'I don't know if the person I'm looking for still lives here.'

'Sure thing, lady. Don't look much like it's a good neighbourhood. I'll wait right here. Go on and knock the door.'

Nora gave him a grateful smile as she mounted the few steps to the front door and knocked. When no-one answered, she knocked again. This time she heard footsteps slowly approaching on the other side. Nora could hear her heart pounding in her chest as the door opened a fraction to reveal an elderly unkempt woman.

'What do you want?' her sullen voice asked. The woman's face was lined like worn leather, her hair greasy and lank, and she held a cigarette in her hand.

'I … I'm looking for my mother,' Nora stammered. 'Her name is Maeve Magill. She wrote to me from here many years ago.'

'Well, she's not here now. I've never heard of her, so go away.' And she turned to close the door.

'Please, is there anyone else here, anyone who might have known her, anyone at all?' Nora's voice trembled, feeling the only link she had with her mother was fading.

'There's no-one else here. I'm the only one left in this stinking hellhole. Your mother's one lucky lady, getting out of here,' the woman cried before shutting the door firmly in Nora's face.

Nora stood, her head bowed as unbidden tears pricked her eyes. 'Are you all right?' the kindly cab driver asked. 'Come on, I'll take you wherever you need to go next.'

'I've got no place to go,' Nora's voice broke. 'I don't know where to go next.'

'Come on, then. I'll take you over to Hallam's place. You're Catholic, right?' he asked. Nora nodded, puzzled as he laughed. 'It's the cross, lady, the cross.'

Within minutes, the cab driver drew up at Father Joseph Hallam's Shelter. 'You'll be safe here,' he said. 'Big Father Joe will sort you out.'

Nora paid the fare, thanked the driver, and walked up to the Shelter. She was quickly shown in to Father Hallam's office. Snow had fallen earlier and the bitter evening now contrasted dramatically with the warm fire burning in the grate.

Father Hallam was a great bear of a man. His face was pockmarked and a long jagged scar stretched from cheekbone to chin. His presence would have been intimidating were it not for the disarming lop-sided grin, which he wore now as he strode into the room to meet Nora, dwarfing the place with his presence. 'Hi, there,' he said. 'Who have we here, then?'

The lost trail for her mother, the loss of her beloved grandfather and the strong, friendly handshake of the priest finally became too much for Nora and she broke down, sobbing as though her heart would break.

'There, there, child. Come on, sit down here and I'll get you a cup of good, strong tea.' Over the next hour, Nora told Father Hallam her story between sips of tea and silent tears. When she had finished, the priest stood up and walked to his desk. 'You'll stay here, then, Nora,' he said. 'This is a big community, but it's still a community and we have many links. You tell me that your mother wrote saying she got your cross at a Mission. That's where we'll start. There aren't too many in the parish she left. I'll make some calls. You go now and get a rest. You can stay in one of the spare guest rooms for a while till we see if we can discover anything.'

Nora thanked him gratefully as he led her to a small room at the top of the hall. She had no sooner laid her head down than she fell into the most restful sleep she'd known since her grandfather died.

***

Over the next few weeks, Nora helped out in the Shelter as Father Hallam called on his contacts for news of Maeve.

By the end of the month, Nora was beginning to despair of finding her mother when the priest unexpectedly called her down to his office. His face was grave and, for a moment, Nora thought that her mother might be dead. 'There's no easy way to say this, Nora. I think I know where your mother is. But if it turns out to be her, she's in pretty bad shape. An old colleague of mine, Father Dan Canning, rang this morning. He had seen the bulletin I circulated in the parishes and thought he might know your mother's whereabouts. But I must warn you, what he told me was pretty grim.

'The Maeve he knew did some volunteer work for him many years ago. She was well liked and was a good worker. She left abruptly one summer, telling Father Canning she had received bad news from home. He discovered later that her mother had died. Maeve fell in with bad company and began drinking; she never returned to her work.

'It was Christmas Eve a year ago when he last saw her. She had many bruises, he said, which she tried to cover up. The man she stays with is a publican with a bad reputation; he had beaten her up pretty bad. Dan tried to persuade her to leave him but his sense was that her spirit was broken. The key to all this, Nora, is that shortly before she left her job, Maeve had bought a silver cross at one of the Mission sales. She told Father Canning she had bought it to send to her daughter, the daughter she had left behind in Ireland. Your journey may be over, Nora.'

Nora thought quietly, *my grandfather told me that this cross would bring me to my mother*. 'Did you get an address, Father?' she asked, aware that she was trembling violently.

Father Hallam left the room, returning with the address a few moments later. 'I'll come with you,' he said.

***

As they stood before the door of the public house, Nora looked up. The publican's name, JP Sheerin, was written across the time-worn frontispiece in fading blue letters. Nora shuddered involuntarily and then braced herself. This was her reason for coming here, her destiny; nothing would stop her bringing her mother home. Father Hallam squeezed her arm reassuringly.

The two entered the dimly lit bar. Tobacco smoke hung in stale, grey, hammocky swathes. Four or five customers sat at the bar. An old woman, merging with the shadows in the corner, looked lazily at the door, her hair yellowed by the smoke. She gently cradled her porter glass as a cat stretched and yawned on her lap.

A gruff, inhospitable voice from behind the bar sliced through the gloom. 'Can I help you?' grunted JP Sheerin as he grumpily folded the sports paper he'd been reading.

'I'm looking for Maeve Magill,' Nora's voice trembled but she fought back the urge to cry.

'Who's asking?' continued the publican.

'This is her daughter,' said Father Hallam, striding purposefully now into the centre of the bar.

The occupants at the bar looked round at the strangers, a moment of interest in their drab worlds.

'Her daughter?' Sheerin laughed, an ugly joyless sound. 'You've got the wrong woman,' he said, 'she hasn't got a daughter.'

The woman who'd been cradling the cat moved up to the bar and, palming a dollar bill onto the counter, said, 'Give us another half, would ye, Mr Sheerin?'

Nora moved into the light, her head high, her voice strong. 'I want to see my mother now.'

The publican drew the pump handle down, sloshing the porter into a grimy glass for his equally grimy patron. He leered at Nora, his steel-grey eyes cold and hard. 'Take a good look, missy,' he pointed to a shape in the corner behind him, 'that's your mother there … or the cat's mother,' he cackled.

Nora moved towards the seated figure which was bent over, half-leaning against the kegs of beer in the corner. She could only see one half of her face but she knew in her soul this was her mother.

'Hey, you!' Sheerin suddenly shouted. 'Get up, there's somebody here to see you.' As the silence seemed to lengthen into forever, the figure in the corner rose awkwardly and shuffled towards the front of the bar.

Nora held her breath as her mother came into sight.

Despite the dark rings beneath her eyes and the ugly yellowing bruise on her temple, it was clear that the woman who stood before her had once been very beautiful. Her dark red hair had lost its lustre and grey streaks fanned her temples. Fire had been replaced by defeat in her now vacant stare; and her full lips were white, almost merging with the deathly pallor of her skin.

Nora moved closer. 'Mother, it's me; it's your daughter Nora.' Maeve Magill now lifted her head slowly, her expression blank and uncomprehending. 'Mother, it's me. I've come to bring you home.'

'Home?' the woman echoed. 'Home? What's that? I've got no home. Here, this is my home!' Shaking her head in confusion, she turned and made her way back to her chair.

'See, what did I tell you? Soft in the head, the stupid cow.' Sheerin laughed out loud.

'Stop that!' Nora raised her voice to the man before her. 'How dare you talk about my mother like that! How dare you treat her like that! My God, what have you done to her?' Her voice tailed off as a welter of emotion took over.

Father Hallam moved forward. 'Maeve,' he said quietly, 'Maeve, this is your daughter Nora. Don't you remember? You told Father Canning about her. Try to remember,' he added gently.

Maeve continued to stare blankly from her chair at the people before her.

'My God, Sheerin, what have you done? I'll see you in gaol for this. You've beaten her once too often,' the priest said as he turned to face the publican.

'What's it to you? She's nobody, just a waste of space. Take your preaching face elsewhere; she's going nowhere, not now, not ever,' Sheerin suddenly hissed and moved out from behind the bar.

'I'm taking her now,' the priest said. 'Come on, Maeve, you're leaving him. I'm going to take you to the Shelter.'

'Get away from her. Get the hell out! She's going nowhere with you, didn't you hear what I said?' Sheerin's eyes looked almost feral in the gloom. Suddenly, he reached behind the bar and drew a handgun. 'Get the hell out of my place now or I won't be responsible for what happens!'

Nora stood rooted to the spot. She felt as though she were a player in some grotesque drama. Her eyes never left her mother. She was aware of the priest moving slowly towards the publican who was pointing the gun straight at him.

'Give me that, Sheerin. Don't be stupid. Come on, give it up.' The other customers now backed away, wary and frightened in the mounting tension. 'Give it to me, man, this is dangerous,' Father Hallam said, still closing in on the angry publican.

Maeve's faltering voice suddenly spoke from the far reaches of the bar, hesitant at first. 'Nora?' Maeve stood up slowly, her eyes locked on her daughter. 'Nora?' she said a second time. Sheerin swung round towards her. 'Nora, can this really be you … my child … my little girl?' She reached forward tentatively.

Seizing the advantage, Father Hallam sprang forward. He grasped Sheerin's arm and was grappling to disarm him when all of a sudden, a yellow burst of flame ripped through the bar as the gun discharged its deadly fire.

Nora sank to the ground as if in slow motion. Everyone at the bar scattered and ducked low in clumsy chaos as a long, sustained wail, like the cry of lost souls, emanated from Maeve. Father Hallam's huge body had pinned Sheerin to the ground now as he shouted to the huddled group on the floor, 'Get the police! Get an ambulance! Hurry, get up, do it! Go, go now!' he commanded. Then, dragging Sheerin across the room, he turned to one of the men, handing him the gun.

'Don't let him out of your sight,' he said breathlessly.

Maeve was holding her daughter's head, her eyes wide with shock and disbelief. 'Nora! Nora! Help her! Please, God, help her!' she cried, imploring Father Hallam, who now stood above them.

Father Hallam bent down, reaching across Maeve to feel for a pulse at Nora's neck. A long sigh slipped from him as he closed his eyes. Placing his hand on her temple, he drew back the hair to reveal a deep graze where the bullet had scorched her skin.

'It missed her, Maeve, it missed. Look, feel her neck,' and Father Hallam took Maeve's hand, guiding it to her daughter's pulse, which was strong and steady. 'You know, this is a brave one, Maeve,' said the priest. 'She wasn't going to give up without a fight. She's come halfway across the world to find you.'

Maeve looked at him, tears of gratitude in her eyes, the hint of light beginning to re-kindle in them. She looked down at her daughter, her hand still at her neck where she fingered the silver cross and, for the first time in the longest time, dared to dream of Ireland and home.

THE INTERVIEW

Kate looked intently in the mirror for the fourth time that morning. It was ten o'clock. Today was the day, the day she had dreaded since the letter arrived – the day of her interview. She posed into her reflection, smiling, tilting her head, and hoping her expression conveyed intelligence to the imaginary faces before her.

Her smile quickly became a frown when she looked beyond her pose to the dark smudges cupping her tired eyes and the sickly sheen of her pallid skin. *Nightmare*, she thought despairingly. *God, I look sick*. Then, flicking impatiently at her hair, two shades darker than her cream blouse, she stood back and pointed resolutely at the mirror. *Stop it, Kate. Come on. Get on with it! Now*, she thought, willing herself forward, *what would make a good opening line?*

'Hello. My name's Kate,' she said breezily, her hand outstretched. *Stupid!* She dismissed the thought. *They'll know that already*.

'Good morning. Lovely day outside,' she smiled widely. *Boring, boring, boring! Come on! Try to be a bit more original*, she urged herself.

An adrenaline surge threatened to overwhelm her as she glanced at the clock again; her interview was scheduled for three o'clock that afternoon.

'Sweet Mother of God help me!' she cried, then stopped suddenly as a light bulb appeared above her reflection in a flash of inspiration. Her mother always lit blessed candles for all of their special intentions and Kate had already booked one for three o'clock. She also remembered her brother saying that interviews always ran late. So with this in mind, she looked confidently into the mirror and delivered her opening line.

'I hope you realise my mother's blessed candle will have burned out by now!' *Brilliant!* she thought, *a perfect start; nice bit of humour, break the ice.*

The shrill ring of the telephone nearly gave her a heart attack. She lifted the phone and, finding her sister on the other side, began to pour out her fears.

'Kate! Calm down!' her sister said. 'Just be yourself. You'll be asked why you want this job – that's bound to be the first question – just speak clearly, you'll be grand.'

Needing more reassurance later, she rang her brother. 'Fire them with your enthusiasm,' he said. 'Always have an answer for why you want the job. It's usually the first question asked, so have a well-prepared answer and you'll be fine. Don't be worrying.'

As he was speaking, Kate glanced in the hall mirror and mentally screamed as she caught sight of her hemline drooping at the front of her skirt. Cutting her brother short with murmured thanks, Kate ran to find her sewing kit and sat down to mend her skirt. As she threaded an impossibly small needle, she went over the job description in her head, backtracking through faded memories of familiar phrases and stringing buzzwords beadlike in her head to store as sparking plugs during her interview. She managed to tack the hemline reasonably well and hoped that the slight puckering in the middle would go unnoticed.

Impressions are everything. Dress well! You'll feel more confident and assured if you're neat and tidy. Don't forget to smile and keep your head up. All the advice of her family echoed through the room, fuelling her anxiety until Kate thought she might go mad. She checked the clock from time to time until, all of a sudden, it was time to go.

Terror was mounting. Kate struggled with the thought that she should have a little drink just to calm herself down. *Please*, she pleaded with herself, *just one*. She wavered. One wouldn't be enough, and any more she might be so relaxed that she wouldn't want to leave. The temptation was powerful, but finally she decided that commonsense would prevail; she needed to be sharp and alert to catch any trick questions.

***

Kate sat in the foyer of the large office block. The worn leatherette chair had seen better days. She had been waiting a few minutes when a small rotund man with a very shiny face emerged from the adjoining room and came over to her, introducing himself as the personnel officer.

'So sorry to keep you waiting, Ms Dayes,' he said, smiling at her.

'Dawes,' Kate replied.

'Does?' the man said searchingly.

'Dawes. You know, as in "Jack"?'

The personnel officer looked at her strangely. Kate felt a warm flush creeping slowly across her chest and was aware that her shoulders were beginning to rise.

'Dawes,' she said again, 'that's my name: Kate Dawes.'

'Oh, I see,' he said, looking relieved. 'Ah, well, just to let you know the interviews are running a little late. But we shouldn't be too long.'

Thank God, she thought, *the interviews are running late. Excellent. A great chance to use my prepared icebreaker. Things are going well so far; it's going to be grand.*

As the minutes passed, however, Kate's anxiety mounted once more. She fidgeted in her seat. Smoothing her skirt with her warm and nervous hands, she realised with dismay that the puckered hemline was more visible now. This was a disaster; she knew that she would be too conscious of her appearance now, which wouldn't help her concentration. Maybe if she turned it round to the side it would look better, or even turn it right around to the back? Or just leave it? She was considering this dilemma when the door opened and the friendly round face smiled at her and uttered the dreaded words, 'We're ready for you now, Ms Dawes. Would you like to come in?'

Kate stood up, remembering at the last minute to adjust her skirt. And in doing so, dropped her handbag, its faulty catch flying open, spilling the entire contents on the floor. Apologising and red-faced, she sank to the ground in an effort to shield the large blue packet of contraceptives from the helpful hands of the personnel officer, who grasped her son's plastic dummy and numerous cosmetic items and thrust them into her hands, reassuring her all the while 'not to worry, not to worry'.

Mortified, she followed him into the interview room. In her emotionally aroused state, Kate's impression was of three blurred figures sitting behind the table. She concentrated on finding the chair and took a few deep breaths as she walked towards the desk.

The middle figure was standing up with his right arm outstretched. Believing that he wanted to shake her hand, Kate reached toward him, only to see his hand withdrawing behind the desk. Realising too late that he was only indicating the chair, she quickly drew back her hand. The chairman, seeing her plight, rose to shake her hand, by which time she had taken her seat. As hovering hysteria threatened to devour her, Kate delivered her practised line.

'I hope you realise that my mother's blessed candle will be burned out by now,' she muttered incoherently.

'Sorry?' queried the chairman with a puzzled expression.

Sweet Jesus! she thought. *They didn't hear it!*

Kate tried to repeat the line, tailing off halfway through before lapsing into silence, an inane expression spreading over her face as she tried to recreate her practised intelligent look.

The chairman coughed politely and glanced apprehensively at the other members of the panel before resuming his seat, taking a deep breath and continuing.

'Well, you're very welcome here today, ah ...' He checked his notes. 'Ms Dawes, isn't it? Sorry about the little mix-up earlier,' he chuckled.

Kate, hearing him laugh, felt that she should reciprocate, but what was intended to be a polite titter erupted into a high-pitched shriek which totally alarmed the chairman, who shot back in his chair.

Kate was appalled by the involuntary sound and instantly fell quiet.

Looking a little shaken, the chairman began again warily.

'Well, as I was saying, Ms Dawes, you're very welcome here today. Now, what do you think this job is all about?'

Kate looked at him as if he had four heads. 'Sorry?' she said.

'Ahem,' he coughed, 'what do you think this job entails?'

The silence in the room was palpable.

'Could I have a drink of water, please?' Kate asked, sweat beading on her forehead as the stalling tactic finally allowed her to respond. 'Don't you mean why do I want this job?' she asked, her voice rising unnaturally.

'Well, no, not just at this point in time. I'm really trying to establish what you understand the job to be all about!'

She looked at the chairman as if he were completely mad. *Speak slowly*, she said to herself, *don't mutter, and look at him.*

'Okay,' Kate muttered, looking at the wall. 'I'm really enthusiastic about this job.'

She stopped short as a glass of water was presented before her. Buzzwords remained frozen, beadlike in her brain, yet to negotiate the communication channels. *Think!* she screamed to herself. *Think!* And then she thought about the water and took a drink. *Help!* She nearly threw up. The water was the fizzy kind and went up her nose, causing her to slam the glass back down on the table and wrench her seat backwards as she spluttered and coughed violently.

'Sorry,' she wheezed as she recovered, 'what was the question again?'

'Why do you want the job?' sighed the chairman.

But it was too late; by this time Kate had despaired of all original thought.

'Well,' she said, 'I'm sorry, I can't answer that question.' *That felt better*, she thought, *more confident.* She drew herself up in the chair, feeling an inner strength as subsequent questions were greeted with the same secretive response: 'Sorry, no, I can't answer that,' until the final question five minutes into her interview and the schedule had completely restored to the set time.

The chairman, visibly bewildered and shrunken in his chair, asked in desperation, 'Are there any questions you would like to ask us?'

'Well, yes, actually, there is one,' Kate said, all sanity now patently gone as a feverish light appeared in her eyes.

'When do you want me to start?'

REDEMPTION

Arlene Gray shivered, pressing her knuckles deep into her eyes and hoping her anxiety would pass. The uneasy feeling was back. She'd had the same sensation the day her little son was killed, and before that, the night she heard her father had died. It was like a sick and scratchy feeling just behind her eyes. *Was she just fanciful? It could be anything*, she tried to reason with herself but she couldn't shake the feeling of apprehension.

'He's back again, Arlene. Get over here,' the needle-sharp voice of her husband John interrupted her thoughts, 'it's definitely him.'

God of almighty! she thought. *What is it now? He's been like a tormented soul all week, pacing back and forth to that window.* She walked slowly over beside him.

'Who's back?' she asked.

'Stratton. I told you I thought I'd seen him last Tuesday. Look,' and he pulled her round, pointing to a hunched figure across the street.

'My God! He's far shook. Are you sure it's him?' She peered closer.

'It's him all right. I wasn't sure last week, but it's him all right. Maybe he was there before, but I didn't notice him. I can't believe he has the nerve to come back here now. Is he trying to rub it into our face?' John's voice was rising.

'I heard he's been dry since the accident,' Arlene said quietly.

'Accident?' roared John. 'Accident, Arlene?'

Arlene took a step back; the circle talk was about to start.

'It's been five years, John. You have to let it go,' she pleaded. 'Anyway, look at him,' she continued, 'he looks worn down, defeated somehow.'

'Good enough for him,' her husband snarled, his broad shoulders hunched up into his neck.

'He's suffered enough, John, God knows. Where's your compassion?'

John swung around to face his wife. 'Same place it was five years ago when he killed my child.'

Arlene stood still. It was useless, she knew, to challenge him. 'My child, too,' she murmured, her wide, dark eyes dimming with sudden grief.

Across the street in the doorway of the County Library stood the object of their discussion: his head was bowed. 'How the mighty are fallen,' sneered her husband.

'Don't, John. Everybody makes mistakes. He—'

'Mistakes!' John flung the word back at her, his derision slapping her silent. 'You know something, Arlene,' his voice quietened almost to a whisper, 'it seems to me you think more about that monster over there than you do about our son.' His eyes narrowed, glittering with anger.

Arlene stared him down, the insult wounding her deeply. 'Tom's dead, John,' she said, a quiet strength in her voice, 'and there's nothing you or I can do about it except treasure his memory.'

Now she reached forward to stroke her husband's head. 'You have to let it go, John,' she said gently. 'If you'd just forgive him, you'd start to feel better. It's the only way to get peace again.' Arlene's voice was soothing, that of a mother to her child, but he shook himself angrily from her touch.

'I'll never forgive him, never! He took our life from us.' John rose from his chair, his face red and contorted. 'As for your Holy Joe advice, forget it,' he laughed with derision. 'Bloody religion! It's all a joke, right up there in the same league as your man's Hippocratic Oath. What a nerve, swearing to preserve life,' he sneered. 'Don't get me started.'

Arlene held back, recognising the start of the soapbox lecture from her husband. She quickly moved to the quiet place in her mind, blocking out her husband's rants, seeing only the ugly twist of his mouth and the spittle-spray of his words.

Her thoughts drifted to the figure across the street.

***

Dr Jonathan Stratton, brilliant surgeon, eminent cardiologist – and, as the papers ran it, functioning alcoholic – had, in one terrible afternoon, written off his car, his wife and six-year-old Tom Gray.

Arlene replayed the scene in her head like an old whirring cinematic reel.

Frame one: Tom riding his bike, John supporting his back. 'Mammy, look at me! Look at me! No hands.'

Frame two: John waving to her with his free hand. 'Just once more round the block.'

Frame three: a silver car, moving too fast, out of control. Arlene screaming. 'Jesus, Jesus! Tom! John, John!'

End of film.

It was the only way she could control the ending.

It was so much worse for John. He saw the car too late as it mounted the pavement, lifting Tom high up into the windscreen and over the top.

'God, give me him back. Dear God, please give me back my son,' he'd cried, Tom's lifeless little body cradled in his arms.

Arlene had mercifully collapsed with shock and it was days before she learned that Mrs Stratton had taken the full force of the connecting lamppost and had died at the scene. Dr Stratton, uninjured, had been jailed for two years but released after eighteen months. He had been asked to take a leave of absence following his release and was eventually encouraged to resign his post, his reputation in tatters.

John had been incensed at the verdict, as had she at the time. But now the thought occurred to her that Dr Stratton's sentence was still being played out.

***

Arlene turned back to the window; she was curious. *Why would the doctor want to return to this place?* 'I hear his son won't let him see the grandchild,' she said, seizing the chance to knock John off his soapbox. 'The little boy must be about four years old.'

'Hell rub it up him,' said John, though a deep sigh had replaced the rant in his voice. *God help me*, he heard from deep within, so unexpected that he almost turned to see who had said it.

Suddenly, Arlene felt she had to get away from the window, away from the house.

Outside, the skies were heavy and leaden. The poor lighting and lugubrious figure of her husband hunched over in the chair suddenly became too much. 'I'm going out a while; might just go into the library for a few books,' she said, pulling on her coat.

When he didn't answer, she closed the door quickly, desperate to breathe fresh air.

Inside, John held his head in his hands. *I'm going to lose Arlene as well*, he thought. *I'm going to lose her, God help me.*

Crossing the road, she walked slowly towards the library. It was colder outside than she'd thought and she noted the tracery of frost webbing the branches in the tree-lined strand. *Winter's only a shiver away*, she thought, recalling a headline from the morning's newspaper.

***

Arlene Gray was only forty-eight years old, although she looked and dressed much older. She had let herself go, gained more weight than was good for her, and yes, she was dowdy, she had to admit. She hadn't always been like that. When she first met John she had been slim and vibrant with dark-blonde hair, which she wore gloriously and loose. John had been the self-professed 'geek' in their class at school, bookish and earnest, always on the periphery of the in-crowd.

She fell in love with his awkwardness. He was tall and lanky, always knocking something over in class or dropping his books. But his arms when they held her like he'd never let go fortressed her very being. It was an intensity that simultaneously exhilarated and disturbed her, that carried them through the years and four heartbreaking miscarriages that culminated in the miracle of Tom.

Until the accident.

That same intensity, dark and brooding now, was slowly but surely strangling any hope for their future.

The last five years had wrung their hearts and souls mercilessly. Arlene had, with the help of her faith, slowly re-emerged; John, an accountant by profession, had buried himself in his work, providing cold financial comfort but little else. Perfunctory and awkward attempts to conceive another child ended in failure … and separate rooms.

That, at least, was bearable, thought Arlene, until these last long months of sick leave as his depression seeped through the house, day after day, relentlessly.

They couldn't go on like this.

***

As she approached the library, her earlier feeling of apprehension grew stronger. She hadn't seen Dr Stratton since the day he had been convicted, when she could not bear to look at him. She had intended keeping her head down as she passed but, at the last moment, she looked up at the figure hunched by the doorway and nodded, 'Nice morning.'

The man looked at her, and in his eyes she could see his physical pain. 'Cold,' he said.

He doesn't recognise me, thought Arlene, at once relieved and vaguely disappointed. 'Not the best of days for standing outside, then,' she persisted, noting his wasted neck within the folds of his greatcoat.

When he didn't answer, she hesitated before moving on into the warmth and silence of the library building. She had the odd sense that an opportunity – of what, she wasn't sure – had passed by.

Outside, Dr Stratton looked up at the sky. His face was grey and heavily lined with brackets either side of his wide thin lips. His high forehead, though, was professorial, and his eyes a deep and striking blue.

Each time he came back to this place, the tableau of his past tormented him. It was all he could do to endure. He had resigned himself to never seeing his son Paul again, or his four-year-old grandson, Robbie, whom he had never met, when he had received a letter unexpectedly.

> Paul needs more time, but I know that he will, in his time, relent. He's a good man, just like his father. I take Robbie to the library every Tuesday now. If you like, you can see him there, but I'm afraid that you can't talk to him just yet …

He'd stopped reading at that point. *The library – could he face returning to that place?*

He could still hear the thud of the child, could see his surprised expression, smell the burning of the twisted tyres and feel his wife's life slip through his hands. Every sense he had was flooded with memory, like barbed wire tearing through his heart.

His son had never forgiven him, but now it seemed he'd been given a second chance, a slim hope of redress, and it was his son's wife, Julie, who had provided the lifeline.

It was almost too late.

It had been three months since the sickness had begun and the pain in his back and abdomen had grown steadily worse. Jonathan knew his time was short.

So he had come back to this place. *A double punishment,* he thought, *not that he didn't deserve it, but it was worth it to see the child.*

Julie, who seemed effortlessly elegant, impressed him, and reminded him a little of his beloved wife, Karen. They shared a subtlety of style; neither, he noted, depended on make-up, such was their natural beauty. The recent visits, although painfully brief, had given him solace. Julie acknowledged him with a slight nod of her head as the child danced and skipped along beside her.

Then, last week, she had stopped as she pushed Robbie ahead of her into the library. 'Next week you can talk to him. I'm telling Paul tonight,' she'd said hurriedly before following her son inside.

Now the day had finally arrived. He glanced up at the clock, stamping his feet on the ground as he blew into his hands. The wind chill seemed to circle him, whipping into his face, icing his bones. It was eleven thirty. He thought he noticed the figure of a man on the other side of the street, staring straight at him. Jonathan looked over, squinting in the weak winter sun, but the man had vanished. He rubbed his eyes and dragged his shoulders deeper into his coat.

Inside the library, Arlene was ambling through the book aisles. She loved reading; it had become her lifeline since Tom's death. She didn't have to think; she could get lost in almost any piece of fiction.

A sudden surge of something, a great sense of peace, shot through her whole being. *What was the matter with her today?* She felt almost buoyant. Her thoughts continued to slip back to Dr Stratton, however much she tried to concentrate on the titles of the teeming books before her on the shelves.

He looks ill, she thought. *God, be kind to him. Let his son reconcile with him. I need to tell him it's okay*, she thought, *I need to do this*. And suddenly it became immediate, *I need to do this now*.

Outside, Jonathan clutched his stomach, a mist of pain fogging his eyes. *Jesus, help me,* he prayed silently as he felt the weakness threaten to overwhelm him.

Across the street, hidden almost in the shadows, Paul Stratton watched his father, his brow furrowed. *What's the matter with him?* he thought. *He doesn't look well … and how did he not see me a moment ago? He was looking right at me. He looks so much older.*

Paul dropped his head. *I should have listened to Julie before instead of being mad at her. She was right, as usual: enough's enough.* He recalled their row.

***

'You did what?' he roared at his wife.

'Don't shout, Paul, you'll upset Robbie.'

'How could you do that? You know I never wanted to see him ever again.'

'He's your father, Paul, the only grandfather Robbie has left. Please, Paul, you have to let go of the past.'

'Never! The great Doctor Stratton thought he was always right. My mother warned him time and time again about drinking and driving, but he was always so cocky. He thought he was invincible.'

'He was a brilliant man, Paul, and your mother loved him. He's paid dearly for his mistakes. Be kind to him. Look, I'm taking Robbie to meet him at the library next Tuesday, why don't you go with us? It'll be easier for you that way.'

'Absolutely not! I'll never forgive him. He's never existed as far as I'm concerned and I forbid you to take Robbie to see him.'

'Listen to yourself, Paul. A bit hypocritical, don't you think? You berate your father for his intransigence but you don't see your own.'

Julie hadn't lost her cool and his anger had dissipated over the days as her words gnawed and ground their way through his conscience.

***

Back in the moment, Paul saw his father look up now as his wife and son turned the corner a few yards from the library door. Julie was walking purposefully towards Jonathan, bending down to Robbie, pointing out his grandfather, just as Arlene came through the doors.

'Doctor Stratton,' she called out, afraid that if she stopped she would lose her nerve. 'Doctor Stratton, you don't remember me. I'm Arlene Gray, Tom's mother …' she began.

Jonathan swung around just as Julie and his grandson reached him.

'I just wanted you to know …' she looked at him now, 'it's important for me to say …' Arlene felt as though she were babbling. 'I know you didn't mean to kill Tom and I know how sorry you feel. I've forgiven you. I'm …' she faltered, overcome by emotion.

Distracted by the unfolding scene, Julie turned to look at Arlene, just as Robbie, dancing by her side, suddenly spotted his father on the other side of the road.

'Daddy!' squealed Robbie. In an instant, the child let go his mother's hand and darted out into the road – directly into the path of an oncoming van.

Horrified, Arlene watched as Jonathan shot into the road, scooping up his grandson in one arm and throwing him to the side of the road and safety, an instant before taking the full force of the van himself.

The screech of brakes merged with the thud and sound of breaking glass. Paul stood, rooted, as Julie ran to comfort her son, who was crying, though unharmed.

'Dad!' screamed Paul.

Jonathan Stratton lay broken on the ground in a dark pool of blood, his life ebbing to a close. The life which had lost all meaning for him was restored now as he felt the tentative hand of his little grandson warm in his, and heard the grateful words of his tearful son: 'I love you, Dad.'

Arlene looked across the street, and through the wintry sky, a single shaft of light illuminated the window where her husband stood, blessing himself over and over, tears streaming down his face, his eyes locked on hers.

CROSSROADS

Caroline bent down, lifted the letter from the mat and turned it over. The name of the building society on the envelope didn't surprise her. She tossed it unopened into the wastebasket, walked purposefully to the kitchen, opened the fridge and took out a bottle of Chardonnay. It was nine o'clock in the morning.

The first sip almost made her retch, but as she quickly finished the glass, the warm glow of the wine worked its magic. She walked over to the telephone and punched in the red flashing button of the answer machine; one message was waiting.

'Hiya, Caroline, it's me. Tried your mobile but you're not picking up, as usual. Anyway, just ringing to let you know the conference didn't finish today as expected, so it's wrap-up time tomorrow. I'll probably be late, so don't wait up. See you. Bye.'

The call was perfunctory. She knew all about Tom's affair and any attempts at discretion were long gone. She wondered how long it would be before he discovered that she'd given up her job, the money in the Master Plan didn't cover the mortgage, she had taken out all her savings, and she was leaving him. She wondered – but she didn't care.

She poured herself another glass, the butterscotch flavours warming and soothing her. She looked at herself in the mirror, itemising each feature like a Saturday shopping list. A fine high forehead, perfectly shaped eyebrows, flawless skin and high, polished cheekbones, oh, and one snub nose, please. She avoided looking at her eyes, windows to her soul; she didn't want to see what was there.

She was thirty-two years old, immaculately preserved, orphaned, childless and soon to be separated. 'Not much going for you, girl,' she said aloud, raising her glass, her mirthless laugh a glacial tinkle in the mausoleum of her home.

She looked around the kitchen; the floor was spotless. Pristine white tiles had been re-washed, dishes were co-ordinated in equal sizes and sat on polished surfaces cleaned at least three times a day. Clinical perfection.

The keys to her car sat on top of a short goodbye letter beside the telephone. A tan leather suitcase sat upright beside the door and in it, all she needed of the last twelve years folded neatly away, nothing of her remaining.

She picked up the ticket from the table and read it aloud. 'Flight NX467 Dublin to Paris, one way.' She revisited an earlier thought: *was she completely mad? She hated flying and she knew no French. What had she been thinking?*

The phone suddenly rang, startling in the silence of the house and, reflexively, she lifted the receiver. 'Hello,' she said sharply.

'Hello. Is this Miss Fisher?'

Her maiden name? No-one had called her that for a long time. 'That's me. Who's this?' She didn't recognise the voice.

'This is Garda Cleary from the station in Cork.'

Caroline wrinkled her brow. 'Yes?' she said uncertainly.

'You have an aunt, a Miss Martha Fisher?'

'Martha?' Taken aback, Caroline reached into her memory, realising she didn't have to travel too far. 'Martha, yes, yes, but I haven't seen her in years. Why? How did you get this number?'

'Ah, your aunt had your name and number in her contacts book. Well, actually, quite a few telephone numbers for you; this was the last on the list.'

'Is she dead?' the stark words were out before she realised.

'No, no, not at all, but I'm afraid she is, well …' he hesitated, 'well, we received a call from a concerned neighbour this morning, who found Martha wandering down the road …'

'And?' asked Caroline.

'And she was wearing no clothes … except for a hat.'

Caroline almost laughed out loud, memories of Martha rushing back. *Naked except for a hat! God, that would be so like her!*

'We had her picked up and taken home, but her doctor thinks she may have to go in somewhere for her own safety. She's not for budging, though. I thought she might have relatives nearer by; do you know of any? There was another number – for a Mrs Grace Fisher – which we tried, but it was disconnected.'

'That was my mother's name, but they weren't in touch.' Caroline was shocked. *Why on earth would Martha have kept her mother's number?* 'Look, is this a joke? I haven't seen Martha for over eighteen years and my mother lost touch with her years ago.'

'Not at all, Miss, not at all. There are no other numbers in the book except for her doctor, the plumber and the like. Do you know of any other relatives?'

'No,' said Caroline distractedly, 'No, she was my father's older sister, much older, actually, never married as far as I know. She stayed with us for a week every summer until …' Caroline took a deep breath.

'Until?' said the Guard.

'My father was killed in a car accident when he was thirty-six; Martha never came back after his funeral. We lost touch after that; my mother never heard from her again.'

'We'll just have to do what we can then. Now, lookit, Miss Fisher, is there any way you could come down here? Her

89

doctor thinks we should strike while the iron's hot, although if you don't want to, I'm sure the social worker here would sign the forms.'

'Sign the forms?'

'To section her,' he sighed. 'She's a risk to herself, a bit off her head, if you know what I'm sayin', but Doctor Piper gave her something to help her sleep and Fran Reedy, that's her neighbour, is doin' the sittin' at the minute. Do you think you could come? That's a Dublin number isn't it?'

'No, God, no. I'm afraid that's impossible. I'm leaving for the airport now; I won't be back …' Caroline hesitated. 'Where do they want to send her?'

'Into Gilmore – sorry, that's the dementia unit – but God knows it'll take some doing. I wouldn't want to be the one who's taking her; apparently she was calling out for you last night.'

'For me? That's ridiculous; I haven't seen her for years,' Caroline said in amazement.

'Well, that's what the neighbour said. Look, are you sure there's nobody else?'

Caroline closed her eyes, 'No, my mother died a few years ago; there's just me.' Her words played themselves back through the sound waves of the phone: *there's just me.* And suddenly she found herself saying, 'Look, give me her address, it'll take me a few hours.' She scribbled down the instructions. 'I'll go by train,' she added, finishing her wine. *Had she gone completely mad?* She didn't know, but she didn't care. *Her life was her own now,* she thought as a great sense of exhilaration swept through her. 'I'll be there as soon as I can,' she said as she lifted her coat and case and without looking back, closed the door on her old life.

***

On the journey down to Cork, Caroline tried to piece together her memories of Martha. She remembered her mother dreading the visits, saying, 'Why doesn't she stay away? She'd wear you out.'

Caroline found herself smiling as she remembered Martha arriving at their door, tooting the horn in the Aladdin's cave that was her car. 'Look at you, Caro; you've grown so big,' as Caroline threw herself into her arms, breathing in the heady mix of patchouli oil and mints.

Then there were the presents: a croquet set with four hammers, hoops and balls; skipping ropes with blue and orange handles; comics and sweets, all for her; brandy and rich tobacco for dad and purple stockings and lace underwear for her mum, who would raise her eyes to heaven and murmur, 'Not wise.'

'Oh, go on with ye, Gracie, doll it up for Jimmy,' she'd say through gales of laughter.

The memories tumbled fast now, with every jerk and jitter of the speeding train.

'She's not the full shilling, Jimmy. God knows, she's nearly fifty; ye think she'd act her age. She has our Caroline's head filled with nonsense.'

And her father's patient and kindly answer: 'Let her be, Grace. She loves her and she's good.'

And I loved her, thought Caroline now as the train whistled past hills and vales towards the city.

'Come on, Caro, get on your coat. We're going to have an adventure.' The destination was always different. Going to the zoo in the double-decker bus where they clattered along the top deck to the front so that Martha could teach her the names of the clouds and trees as they passed; altostratus was her favourite cloud formation. 'Come on, Caro, what do they look like to you?'

'Ice cream tears? Sea waves?'

'Good girl,' she'd say, clapping her hands. 'That's it, use your imagination.'

Then there were the long hot days on the beach – kelp became mermaid's hair; seaweed, chocolate octopus. All the stones and shells were diamond accessories to the great pink bosom of sand at the edge of the wrinkled sea. And the park – Martha in her striped socks and long velvet coat, flying down the banana slide, then jumping off to catch her, swinging her around in the air. She was like a summer's dance at a crossroads, free and wild and wonderful, a torrent who swept in and out of their lives.

Her poor mother never got used to it, her quiet, ordered life turned on its head for fourteen days every summer. 'That's the last time she's coming, Jimmy,' she told him every year. 'I'm not fit for it.'

Until it really was the last time, the time when her father had died.

'I won't be back for a while now, Caroline,' she said, 'but don't forget me; you're my special spirit,' she whispered before leaving in a swirl of purple.

She hadn't heard from her since until now.

**

It was nearly two o'clock by the time the train pulled into the station at Cork.

Caroline checked the address – Avoca, Linden Lane, Bantry. *Another journey, but what a special one,* she thought, stepping onto the bus and drinking in the beauty of the southwest of Ireland in all its magical splendour.

By the time she reached Bantry, all thoughts of leaving Ireland had disappeared: her heart was here. She reached for her case, suddenly buoyant, thanked the bus driver and hailed a taxi.

92

'How's it going?' asked the cab driver cheerfully as he noted the address. 'Old Martha's place?'

'Yes,' said Caroline, 'she's my aunt. You know her, then?'

'Martha?' He laughed, a deep belly sound, 'She's quite a character. I wouldn't say that there's too many round here that don't know her.'

When Caroline arrived at the house she was met by the harassed neighbour, who looked as though she hadn't slept in weeks. A thin-lipped, sharp-featured woman, she held out her hand to Caroline. 'You must be Miss Fisher. I'm Fran Reedy; the Guards said you were coming down.' Caroline shook the roughened hand as the woman continued, 'She's in her bed; quiet at the minute. Well,' she raised her eyes to heaven, 'God alone knows how long that'll last. So, you're her niece?' she asked Caroline, who realised by the tone that judgment was being brought to bear.

'Yes, yes I am, but I haven't seen Martha for more than eighteen years or so. She moved addresses when I was young and we lost touch.'

Fran Reedy raised a sceptical eyebrow. 'Is that so?' she said. 'When you were young, you say?'

'Yes. When I was fourteen, actually.' Caroline felt an irrational need to defend herself.

'Hmm,' the neighbour folded her arms. 'Well, you're here now, I suppose. She'll need dressed in a while and the doctor said he'll call back. Can't be up to this anymore, she's a bloody liability.' And with that, Fran Reedy shook her thin frame through the door and started up the path.

What a targe! thought Caroline, unsure now what to expect as she quickly followed.

The bungalow was a quirky mix of odd-shaped rooms, low beams, and recesses teeming with books. Multicoloured throws covered the comfortable armchairs, which faced into the antique fireplace. And then Caroline stopped dead. On the fire-brace wall she saw herself smiling down from her graduation photograph. 'Where on earth …?' she began, a strange feeling creeping over her. 'How did this get here?'

Caroline shook herself and took a deep breath before moving to the bedroom. She hesitated slightly, knocking gently before entering. She could see Martha from the doorway and edged up to the bed, the silence in the room unnerving her. Martha lay in the foetal position, her silver hair knotted in a thin plait down the curve of her back. Her skin was stretched taut over her fine cheekbones and a dark purple bruise leaked out from beneath her hairline.

Caroline reached forward to pull the sheet around her just as Martha stirred. 'Martha, it's me,' she whispered. Martha's eyes opened, the intensely blue, almost violet colour unmistakable, like her father's eyes and her own as well. 'Yes, it's me, Martha.' Caroline looked at the blank eyes in front of her. *God, what am I thinking? Martha won't know me. It's been so long, eighteen years … but the graduation photograph?* 'It *is* me, Martha, it's Caroline,' she said, reaching gently for her hand. The papery skin was like a transfer on a map of knots and bone.

'Caroline?' The voice when it came shot right through Caroline. It was so distinct, as though it had been preserved in a hidden recess somewhere within the passage of time. 'Caro,' she said now more urgently, her grip surprisingly strong around Caroline's hand, 'where am I?'

'You're home, Martha, in your own bed. It's okay.' But her words were lost as Martha slipped back into her deep, sedated sleep.

Caroline pulled the quilt up over the thin shoulders before wandering out into the main room. She was drawn again to the photograph, trying to make sense of it all. *Who had sent this to Martha? It could only have been her mother.* She looked around the room. Over by the latticed window, an old desk with an array of tiny drawers faced out onto the large gardens. Beyond lay nothing but verdant, rolling hills. The place was beautiful, peaceful.

An untidy sprawl of paperwork adorned the desk, manuscripts of scribble, a buff bulky folder of private papers and an old photograph album with gold leaf on the pages. Curious, Caroline opened the first page to the circled frames of an elderly couple sitting straight backed and stiff as their Victorian clothes. *Her great-grandparents?* Page after page was a methodical chronology of family. Pictures of her own grandparents – she knew these from her father's photographs. Then came Martha as a young child, as a schoolgirl and as a young woman. She was exceptionally beautiful. Even then there was a hint of devilment in those extraordinary eyes. Then Caroline's father, in his neat little sailor suit; Martha, an awkward teenager, stood with a protective arm around him.

She turned the pages slowly, fascinated by the discovery of her family line. Her father's graduation and his wedding day. Caroline had seen photographs of her parents' wedding day before, but not this one. She studied her father's fine, handsome face, his eyes like the vivid rings of a blue Saturn. He had been the world to her.

Then she moved to her mother. Grace was small, with dark red hair and eyes the colour of amber, eyes which seemed to Caroline to have a hint of defiance as she linked her arm proprietorially to her new husband. Martha was at his other side just like a best man, her long blonde hair cascading down from beneath a wide-brimmed hat. She was as tall and large boned as Caroline's mother was fine.

Caroline turned the pages then and sat back in the chair.

Caroline, at six weeks, Caroline at one year, all photographs numbered and dated. Photographs of Martha and her at their home in Dublin.

Then, turning the last page, Caroline gasped aloud: her graduation day, photographs from her gap year in New Zealand, her wedding. Caroline didn't understand. *Who had sent her these? Her father, maybe, in the early years? But after that?* And again, she wondered about her mother. She knew Grace didn't have much time for Martha, and as far as Caroline knew, they had lost touch in those years after her father's death. A sharp knock startled her and sent her hurrying to open the door.

'Doctor Piper … here to see Martha,' he said as he breezed and wheezed into the house. Caroline hoped that her first impression of the man didn't register on her face. He must have been at least twenty stone. *Not a good advertisement for any health service,* she thought, *and he had a surprisingly high-pitched voice for such a large man.*

She held out her hand. 'I'm Martha's niece, Doctor Piper: Caroline.'

'Good, good. Martha will be happy,' he said with a hearty handshake.

'You've known Martha long, Doctor?' asked Caroline, following him into the bedroom.

'She's the reason for my lack of hair,' he said, though not unkindly, 'and many sleepless nights these past few months. I really think, dear, she'd be better off in a place where she can have all the care she needs.' He looked down at Martha peacefully asleep and raised a thick white eyebrow. 'Well, I'm glad to see her asleep; she needed the rest. Now, I've made arrangements,' he said, guiding Caroline outside to the living room as he lowered his voice. 'Do you think you could take her? It would be better if she went in voluntarily,' he said, opening his case to give Caroline a letter. 'Just hand this in with her when you arrive. They're expecting her.'

Caroline backed away, her arms raised before her, looking at him in alarm, 'Sorry, no way, Doctor. It's been years since we've seen each other, I couldn't ...' Dr Piper glanced at the graduation photograph on the wall. 'I couldn't ...' Caroline insisted. 'Besides, is it absolutely necessary?'

'Look, dear,' he said patiently, 'your aunt has been almost knocked down, almost died from hypothermia, almost bled to death following a drinking binge where she ended upside down behind the toilet bowl, having split her head on the cistern.' Caroline searched his face for signs of exaggeration, finding none. 'She needs care,' he said. 'I like Martha. She's a great old spirit, but her luck is running out, I'm afraid. She could wander off again tomorrow.' He took his handkerchief out of his pocket and mopped his brow. 'Recently, she seems to be searching for somebody and I think the neighbour is finding the responsibility a bit much. She talks about you often, you know,' he added as he closed his case.

'I just don't get that, Doctor. Is that part of her condition? I'm telling you it's been eighteen years.'

'Eighteen years to a child is a little different to us oldies,' he smiled. 'Besides, you're really the only family she has.'

'Is she likely to get better?' asked Caroline.

'No. I'm sorry to be so blunt, but last week she was found up at the cemetery putting a blanket on a child's grave. I'm afraid it won't be long before she'll retreat into that little world of her own permanently. Well, I have to go on. Look, here's my number. Ring me if you have any problems and I'll come over. I hope you can talk her round, em, Caroline, isn't it?' She nodded. 'Okay, ring me if you need me, Caroline,' he said as he waddled past her like a huge toby jug.

'Thank you, Doctor,' she said, her anxiety growing. *This was a mistake,* she thought, *she should never have come.* She felt trapped now. *What should she do? God, she felt like a drink!* She wanted to open the door and run. This hadn't been the life she'd envisaged, but then to be fair, that hadn't been thought through either. *She couldn't leave – not yet. But*

97

to take Martha into a home? Caroline walked back into the bedroom and over to the wardrobe. *Maybe she should get some clothes ready?*

She almost laughed out loud. The red velvet coat, striped jerseys and long multicoloured skirts hung beneath a shelf with an assortment of oddly shaped hats of all colours and sizes.

'Caroline, is it really you?'

Caroline swirled around guiltily. 'Martha, you're awake. How are you feeling?'

'Are they putting me away?' Her eyes were clear and she was calm, alert and comprehending.

Caroline bit her lip and knelt down beside the bed. 'The doctor thinks it might be good for you to go into a place where you can get some care, Martha. He's worried about you,' she said gently.

'Worried, my arse,' she said. 'He's worried I'm going to outlive him, that's all; probably has a flutter on with the bookie.'

Caroline did laugh out loud this time; this was the woman she remembered. 'I can't believe I'm here,' she said. 'Why didn't you keep in touch?'

'I couldn't, not after your father died. Took me a long time to get over that.' She coughed. Caroline reached to the bedside table for the glass of water as Martha pulled herself up in the bed with difficulty. 'It's that bloody sedative,' she said. 'Where was I?'

'You were talking about Dad.'

'Jimmy,' she sighed for the longest time. 'Yes, Jimmy. After the funeral, Gracie said she thought it would be better if I didn't come back for a while, you know, to give you both time, so I asked her to send me on photographs of you from time to time. I sent you letters as well.'

Caroline sat back on her shoes, shocked. 'What?' she said with surprise.

'Yes, well, I can see by your face you didn't get them, but at least she sent the photos, I'll give her that. You were all I had left of Jimmy, you see.' Martha suddenly sat forward. 'It's cold out there. Do you think he'll need a blanket?'

'What? Who?' Caroline looked confused.

'Jimmy. Do you think he'll need a blanket?' Martha pulled off the covers and tried to drag herself from the bed, her eyes full of fear.

'Martha, it's all right, it's all right.' Caroline got to her feet, alarmed by the change in Martha's face.

'Get away from me! Who are you? I don't know you,' she wailed. 'He hated the dark. Dear Jesus, he'll be freezing. Give me my clothes over – give me over my clothes.' Martha began clawing at the bedclothes, her thin long body straining against the sheets.

Then, just as suddenly, she stopped and lay back against the pillow. 'Caroline, help me. I need to get ready.' Her voice was resigned.

'What should I do?' Caroline was still shivering from the transition she had just witnessed.

'Just help me get dressed,' sighed Martha.

'It's all right, it's all right,' Caroline soothed.

'Lately, I don't know, everything just seems to be in a fog. Maybe Piper's right,' she said, patting Caroline's hand. 'Maybe it's time. Give me a hand here, Caro, I've been long enough in the pit today. Anyway, tell me about you.'

'Nothing much to tell,' said Caroline, avoiding the penetrating eyes as she gently pulled the nightdress above Martha's head.

'Come on, Caro, it's me. Remember?'

And so as she helped dress Martha in warm layers of coloured cottons and a long over-tunic of dark pink wool, Caroline told her story. As she unbraided Martha's soft white hair, all the pain and loneliness of her marriage loosened like the silver ripples now flowing over the bent and narrow shoulders before her. Martha sat on the side of the bed, her eyes closed.

When Caroline had finished, Martha looked up at her with a fierce expression of pride. 'You are magnificent, Caro, to turn your life around like that. I'm so proud of you. Jimmy would have been very proud,' her eyes clouded. 'I loved him, you know; nobody ever knew how much.'

'I know, Martha, and he loved you. He told me stories of how you'd fight all the boys in the street if they so much as looked sideways at him.'

Martha laughed a queer guttural sound. 'Did he tell you that?' she said. 'Here, help me up off the bed, Caro.' She walked slowly over to the window, her back stooped, and looked up at the sky, 'Look, Caro, altostratus,' she said. 'Do you remember?'

'How could I forget, Martha? They were great days – every one an adventure.'

'Yes, great days. God, I wish I could still drive! I would take you away now up to the mountains, way up behind Glengariff to Healy Pass.' She rubbed her head with her hand. 'But I don't seem to know how any more; it's all topsy-turvy. Do you drive, Caroline? You can have my car, you know, the keys are hanging behind the door. Maybe you and Jimmy could come and visit me again.' She shook her head as though she were trying to free something. 'But what am I saying? Jimmy's dead, isn't he?' She looked uncertainly at Caroline. 'Lord, I need a drink.' She pointed to the wardrobe. 'Go on, child, take out that bottle of whiskey in there.' Caroline rummaged around the shelf until she found the bottle. 'Old Piper doesn't know about this one,' Martha winked, and despite her growing concern for Martha's state of mind, Caroline smiled. 'Come on, get two glasses, Caro. I want to show you something.'

Martha reached forward to the desk by her window and brought out an old black-and-white mounted photograph in a silver frame in which Martha was holding a baby in her arms.

Caroline poured the whiskey into the glasses and then lifted the photo to look at it closely. 'Is that my father?'

'That's your father, Caro. Isn't he beautiful? Do you see? Do you see, Caroline?'

'See?'

'Look closely, Caro,' she said. Caroline looked at Martha, confused. *What was it she wanted her to see?* She scanned the photograph again: her father, just newborn, his tiny hand crooked around Martha's little finger. Caroline lifted her gaze to the picture of Martha, who was looking down at the child. There was something about her eyes. Caroline looked more closely. Such an exquisitely tender expression of love. *Almost like,* she thought … Caroline shook her head … *don't be stupid,* but the thought persisted, *almost like a mother.*

Caroline started. Looking up at Martha, then down again at the photograph, and a sudden, shocking realisation dawned. 'He's yours! He's your son!'

'He never knew,' she nodded, 'and neither did your mother. My father worked in the Registry Office. Easy to arrange the details on the birth certificate; couldn't be done now, thank God,' she said sadly, 'but it was best that way. I was fifteen years old. I suppose I should have been grateful to my parents – they could have sent me off to one of those convents and I would have lost him forever.'

Caroline said nothing, her mind in a mill of emotion.

Martha took another long, slow drink, draining the glass. 'Lovely,' she said, closing her eyes. 'Pour me another. At least when I go, I'll be in my cups '

Caroline refilled the outstretched glass, then walked into the living room. Her head was teeming with thoughts. *What should she do? Could she do it?* She reached for the doctor's letter and studied the name and directions of the home before putting it into her pocket. Then she returned to the bedroom. Martha sat in the chair, a half-smile on her face, her whiskey finished. She had taken the photograph from the frame and was working a letter free from behind the mount. 'Will they put me away do you think, Caro?'

'Not as long as I'm about, Martha,' she said, her decision made. 'Now, let's get you into your coat and we'll go for a drive.'

'This is for you, Caro,' said Martha, handing her the letter. 'I don't know if I'll remember where I'll put this again, so I'm giving it to you now.'

'What is it?' asked Caroline.

'It's my will,' said Martha.

'Martha?'

'Go on, read it.'

Caroline opened the letter slowly and began to read: 'Last Will and Testament of Martha Fisher.' Caroline looked at Martha, but she was looking out the window. 'I, Martha Fisher, being of sound mind—'

'Well, now and again,' interrupted Martha with a little laugh, 'but I think it's valid.'

Caroline continued, '. . . do hereby leave all my worldly possessions to Caroline Fisher, daughter of my beloved Jimmy and his wife, Grace Fisher, to do whatsoever she pleases as long as it's not conventional. Signed, Martha Fisher. Witnesses: John Vale, Solicitor; Bill Piper, Medical Doctor.'

'It's for you and Jimmy,' she said, though her voice was wavering, unsure, a quizzical look in her eyes. 'Jimmy – was that his name? It sounds funny in my mouth.'

Caroline gently lifted her glass. 'Come on, Martha, we're going out now.'

The big old Chrysler started beautifully and Caroline

followed the signs into the town and beyond. They had travelled two miles when they came to a crossroads. Caroline stopped and took the envelope Dr Piper had given her from her pocket, reading the address before tearing it into tiny pieces.

To the left lay Skibbereen. She looked to the right; a small signpost read, Gilmore Nursing Home, 5 kilometres. Martha was humming quietly beside her with her eyes closed. The signpost straight ahead read, Glengariff and Healy Pass.

'Are you up for an adventure, Martha?'

'Up to the mountains?' her face was animated, shining.

'Up to the mountains,' Caroline laughed. It wasn't going to be easy, but then who needed easy?

***

The golden countryside lay wide open, far from the misery and frenetic world she had left behind. She opened her bag and took out her mobile phone: eleven missed calls from Tom. Caroline smiled to herself. She eased the big car forward, then rolled down her window and in one liberating, sweeping arc, threw her phone far up into the blue of the West Cork sky.

THE CURE

'Put yourself into God's hands,' the old priest said as he took Ellie's hand and looked deeply into her eyes. Her expression was desolate as she sat in her wheelchair, her right arm and leg useless and heavy, her speech, once vibrant and witty, silent now these past two years.

Annie had taken her Aunt Ellie to see Father Thornton, who was renowned for his healing ministry and having a 'cure'. She wasn't convinced but hoped that Ellie would derive some sense of inner peace, even if she wasn't mended of her stroke. She watched now as a silent tear spilled down her aunt's pale cheek and felt her own emotions threaten to overwhelm her.

The old priest said nothing more and after a few moments of quiet prayer, he guided them to the door.

On the journey home, Ellie gestured for Annie to open the window. She seemed faint and began to gasp for breath at an alarming rate. Annie stopped the car and ran to open the passenger door to give her some air. She reached for a bottle of water in her bag and, with difficulty, managed to get her to drink a little, which seemed to revive her. The effort of this, however, had exhausted her and by the time Annie got her home, Ellie was only semiconscious.

Within hours of calling the doctor, Ellie now lay in the darkened bedroom, gravely ill.

Annie was musing about the words of the old priest and, despite being a sceptic, could not help but wonder at the coincidence. *This was her cure*, she thought. *Ellie was being healed through death.*

Doctor Phillips, the family GP, came into the room just then.

'How do you think she is, Doctor?' Annie said in a low voice as she noticed her mother dozing by the bedside.

'She's very ill, Annie. How long has it been since her last stroke?'

'Two years this March, Doctor. She's never spoken a word since as you know.'

'Tragic,' he said. 'It was an unusually dense stroke, but I'm afraid this second one has been catastrophic. It's highly unlikely that she will regain consciousness. You know, Annie, I'm glad for Ellie. She's endured a long sentence locked in this silent world.' The doctor dropped his voice. 'Your mother refuses to sign her in for full-time care, as she wants to look after her herself, but I shouldn't think it will be too long in any case.'

As the doctor left the room, Annie gently shook her mother. She looked down at the soft, downy cheek and felt a sudden surge of love for her. 'You go and lie down, Mum, and I'll stay here. I'll call you if anything happens. Go on, you're exhausted. I'll wait with Ellie.'

Annie took up the vigil by the bedside, gently mopping Ellie's brow. The day was drawing to a close and Annie moved to the window to draw the curtains. As she was returning to the bedside, her foot caught an upturned edge of the carpet and she fell heavily against the side of the wardrobe. She rose quickly, rubbing her shoulder and glancing over at the bed. However, Ellie remained in a deep sleep.

The force of the fall had opened the door of the wardrobe and an old shoebox had been dislodged from the inside shelf. As Annie lifted it to put it back, she noticed inside a small bundle of cream envelopes tied with a blue ribbon. Curious, Annie lifted them up and examined the writing on the front: Miss Eleanor Ross, the line read, in fine, spidery writing. *The full title*, thought Annie, smiling.

Ellie had been Christened Eleanor, but for as long as Annie remembered, she had been called Ellie, despite her protestations that Eleanor was much more fitting for a lady such as herself.

Annie was about to put the letters back when the postmark caught her eye – Dublin. She glanced at Ellie just as she gave an audible sigh and shifted slightly in the bed.

Annie untied the little bundle and cautiously drew out the first envelope. She turned it over in her hand, examining the front and then the reverse, where she noticed the letters M and E intertwined.

Intrigued, Annie slowly drew the letter from the envelope. Feeling a little guilty, she glanced up once more at Ellie – and nearly fell off the seat. Her aunt's eyes were wide open and staring straight at her. Shocked, Annie dropped the bundle of envelopes to the floor. Just as suddenly, Ellie's eyes closed and Annie put her hand to her head, her heart hammering in her chest.

After composing herself, Annie retrieved the letters, then moved to the other side of the bed, having first ensured Ellie was comfortable. 'Do you mind if I read one, Ellie?' she whispered to her aunt. She hoped that Ellie had heard, even if she couldn't answer. Annie scanned the letter.

Eleanor,
I couldn't believe it when I saw you on the train today. It has to be destiny of some sort. We have seen each other only four times, yet each time I am completely overwhelmed by you. I hope it is the same for you. You didn't see me at first today and I had the chance to watch as you took your seat and made yourself comfortable for the journey. Eleanor (I could write your name a thousand times), you are so lovely. You shook your glorious auburn hair, shiny like a chestnut fresh from its case, when you

removed your hat and I just thought how perfect you are, so very beautiful. The silliest of things: you began to take off your gloves. I watched as you looked out the window with a little secret smile on your face and I hoped you were thinking of me …

Annie looked up from the sheet, feeling her face redden. She felt a rush of guilt and hastily replaced the letter in the envelope, carefully tying the bundle again. She moved back to the other side of the bed, facing Ellie in wonderment.

***

Ellie had worked in the Civil Service for thirty years before she had been cut down by a stroke at the premature age of fifty. Her work took her to many parts of the country, mainly to Dublin, but also visiting farmlands and customs offices.

She was only four foot eleven and compact, having tiny, proportionate hands and feet, a delicate little nose, small ears and lovely, oval, light-brown eyes. She was a talented artist with an extraordinary soprano voice reminiscent of Deanna Durban. She had never married.

Lawrence, her first love, had died tragically in a road traffic accident on his way to collect her from work. Ellie had never lost her sense of guilt and for many years didn't go out of her house at all.

Her health had always been precarious, as she had suffered rheumatic fever as a child. She loved travel and it was on a long flight to America that the first signs of heart trouble were detected, leading to open-heart surgery. The operation had been successful, but in the ensuing weeks, Ellie had become withdrawn and depressed. Annie tried to recall the sequence of events.

Ellie had lived with them for as long as Annie could remember. She remembered the summer following the surgery when Ellie returned to work and attributed this to the positive change in her aunt's mood. She travelled back and forth to Dublin during these months and each time, Annie now recalled, she was like a new person on her return. It was strange how clearly the pictures of those last nine months of Ellie's *normal* life now seemed.

Small memory windows emerged: Ellie singing in front of the large, bevelled hall mirror as she combed through her lovely hair; Ellie laughing with Annie's mother, head thrown back at some shared observation; Ellie lying on the carpet in front of the fire, looking so young as, lost in her thoughts, she stared deep into the flame, her cheeks rosed by the heat.

***

Annie looked tenderly at her aunt and silently thanked God for having given Ellie someone special with whom to share her great capacity for love.

It had been the following March when, without any warning, Ellie had been struck down with a blood clot to her brain, which had resulted in the stroke. *Stroke*, Annie mused, *such a gentle word for such a devastating condition.*

Annie looked at Ellie's face again. She seemed more relaxed; her breathing was easy and her eyes closed now in peaceful sleep. Unable to hold back her curiosity any longer, Annie took another letter from the bundle and began to read:

Eleanor,
Such a beautiful place you took me on my recent journey North. I hadn't been to this part of Inishowen before.

Walking up the bramble lane to the cottage was idyllic. The sweet fragrance of the wild woodbine above the burn is still with me. Do you remember you plucked a little sprig and held it against your brow? I watched as you carried it for a while, pointing out the road through the hills to the mysterious valley of the Holy Well and Mass Rock. As we rounded the bend to the 'Bushes', the old thatched cottage of your childhood summers, you dropped the flower and I lifted it into my pocket. It is a little piece of you, my love, that I carry everywhere. Thank you for the gift of sharing your childhood home with me. The spring by the mountain heather and the views of that beautiful Lake of Shadows, Lough Swilly, were breathtaking. I will wear the memory of that place against my heart in the cold winter nights.

I'm sitting here this evening at my desk. Lena is in one of her black moods. This morning I found her crying at the bottom of the stairs where she'd fallen. Her nightdress was ripped and stained from a small, bloody gash on her head. The whiskey glass had shattered beside her and she was scooping what was left of the drink into her hand, disregarding the broken slivers of glass. She flew into a rage when I suggested that we should get a doctor to look at her wound.

I finally persuaded her back to bed and washed and bandaged her head as best as I could. I can hear her now, pacing the floor above. She's restless and knows that there's no drink left in the house. It's going to be a long night.

But you, dear Eleanor, you, my love, how you sustain me in these times. As I write this, your beautiful spirit warms and restores me …

Annie looked up quickly as Ellie sighed audibly, but her aunt was sleeping – peacefully, it seemed. The third and fourth letters told more of the life of Ellie's friend. His name was Michael, she learned, and he was a senior civil servant, like Ellie. He had been married for twenty years and devoted to his wife, though she had long been a hopeless alcoholic. What struck Annie from his writing was his loyalty to her. He spoke of her with tolerance and compassion yet his sadness flowed through every line as he wrote of his love for Ellie.

Annie reached for the last letter and took it out. As she did, a smaller, brown envelope fell out of the main packaging. She left it aside as she read Michael's words:

Eleanor,

How I wish I had met you earlier, my darling Eleanor. It is so unfair to you that I can only offer you my love from a distance. When we are together, it is all I can do to restrain my physical need of you. I dare not cross the line; if I do, I know there would be no stopping. I've got nothing to give, Eleanor. It's hopeless. I can't leave Lena, especially now she is to go into hospital tomorrow. I've taken your advice at last, Eleanor, and confided in my doctor. He says her brain has been affected; she becomes more violent by the day. Last night, she broke two windows at the bottom of the stairs with her fist. It's a miracle she didn't cut herself more seriously. Lena needs more help than I can give her. I haven't been fair to her, trying to conceal things for so long. I should have sought help for her earlier. I will try to

Annie was puzzled by the abrupt ending of the letter and realised he hadn't finished it. She turned it over, but the back was blank. She remembered the brown envelope then and picked it up, turning it over as she did. In large capitals, the word BITCH screamed at her. Almost simultaneously, Ellie's eyes flew open and Annie fell back in the chair.

When she recovered from the shock, she leaned forward and whispered to Eleanor. 'Ellie, Ellie, you're awake. Are you okay?'

Ellie's face was ghostly as she looked at Annie, then very deliberately looked down at the letter in Annie's hands.

'What is it, Ellie? Will I open it?'

Ellie nodded almost imperceptibly. The date was written at the top of the envelope: 23 March.

Annie frowned; she struggled to capture a memory, one just beyond her reach. *The twenty-third of March; why was that so familiar?* She opened the letter and began to read, the opening lines startling her beyond belief:

You crafty little tramp! You didn't know I knew about you, did you? Well, it's all over now. You see, he never was going to leave me for you. Did you really think he would, you stupid tramp? Oh, I knew all right, knew from the first day he met you. He was different when he came back. Tired, he'd said, when I asked him where he'd been. He just said he was tired and went to bed. I knew he'd met someone, knew by the look on his face. I watched him after that. I saw him in his study and a smile on his face as he would pretend to write reports. But I knew it was to you.

He put me to bed tonight as usual and brought me up some tea, all sweetness and light. But he couldn't bluff me, not tonight, not after I heard him talking to the doctor, wanting to put me away. I knew his game. I crept down behind him to his study. He was writing, then leaned back on his chair as he took out something from his drawer. I waited to see and then he turned around and I could see that it was a flower of some sort. I nearly screamed when I saw him kiss it, then put it back in the drawer and start to write again.

I could not take it any more. I confronted him then and there. He was startled and just stood looking at me, saying nothing. He tried to tell me I wasn't well! Me! Such a laugh! Tried to get me to go back to bed. I wasn't going to fall for that again. I ran to the desk and got out the precious flower and tore it in front of him. And still he stood there. Only when I promised that I would make sure that YOU would suffer, did he say anything. He came towards me, telling me that I was wrong! But I ran past him, upstairs with the letter. He came after me, but I was too quick. He'd nearly reached me at the top when he missed his footing and fell. Broke his neck. He never got to finish the letter, but I kept it and an envelope he'd already addressed so I could send it to you. He's DEAD. So now, you can go to hell, TRAMP!

Annie dropped the letter in disbelief. She reached out to Ellie, wanting to lift her up and cradle her. She had been so maligned.

Suddenly, she gasped in shock as realisation dawned. The date of the letter was 23 March. Ellie would have received the letter two days later, 25 March. *The day she took the stroke.*

Annie closed her eyes and could only imagine the devastating and terrible shock her aunt must have received, especially when she read what was pinned to the letter – an obituary notice:

Kavanagh, Michael, 55 years.

Suddenly. As the result of an accident at his home. Dearly beloved husband of Lena. Funeral procession will leave his home tomorrow 12 March to St Vincent's

112

Church for Requiem Mass and immediately afterwards to Glasnevin Cemetery. Loved and will be so sorely missed by his devoted and sorrowing wife.

Annie looked at Ellie, tears in her eyes. Ellie was animated now and agitated. She gestured to Annie with tremendous determination. It was a familiar gesture, recognised by Annie over the past two years: Ellie wanted to write.

Annie held her breath as she watched the colossal effort made now by Eleanor. After what seemed an eternity, Annie took the page from her aunt. In shaky, almost indecipherable writing, Ellie had written the word BURN.

'You want me to destroy the letters, Ellie?' Annie asked.

Ellie, exhausted by the monumental effort, nodded weakly, then gave a long sigh. At once, her breathing began to change. Her colour flushed, then paled again. Her head turned to the side. Ellie's eyes were open, but this time she looked beyond Annie towards the window. A deathly rattle sounded from her chest.

Annie stayed stock-still. She knew Ellie was dying. She watched, frozen, as her aunt lifted herself up in the bed, pointing towards a spot behind Annie, with a radiant smile on her face.

Just as gently as she had arisen, Ellie sank, as if in slow motion, back to the pillow and softly breathed her last. The peacefulness of her passing echoed the peace that now came upon Annie as she felt a great sense of being blessed by the witness of Ellie's death and the miracle of her cure. There would be time enough to call her mother.

She leaned over to kiss Ellie, resting her cheek on her forehead. Her eye caught the fine gold chain with the delicate Claddagh lying on the now-still breast. Reaching over, Annie turned it round to see what she now knew she would see – the letters M and E intertwined within the heart.

VEIN GLORIOUS

Very handsome, she thought, watching the boy.

'Anvil? Sickle? Dark Angel?' they shouted.

'Not bad,' he smiled.

The game was novel, she supposed, if a little puerile.

'Our glorious Soviet Republic!' shouted a gleeful Sergei triumphantly.

'Good, comrade, but too conventional. I need originality,' said the boy.

'The South Eastern United States of America?' a small voice ventured.

As the jeers erupted, she came before him. Gently she ran her fingers across the silk of his scalp, caressing his mysterious mark with gossamer grace. Heat stirred in his loins as she worked her way along the definition of his birth. Silence throbbed in the room.

'So,' he said, his voice teasing, inviting, 'you have an answer?'

'A bleeding chicken?' she smiled disarmingly.

He threw back his head, roaring with laughter. 'Excellent, comrade, you win. What is your name?'

'Raisa,' she said. 'And yours?'

'Mikhail,' he said, stretching forth his hand.

The micro story *Vein Glorious* was first published in *Wonderful World of Worders*, 2007, by Guildhall Press.